Also by Steve McCondichie:

Lying for a Living

The Parlor Girl's Guide

Share Your Thoughts

Want to help make *The Parlor Girl's Guide* a bestselling novel? Consider leaving an honest review on Goodreads, your personal author website or blog, and anywhere else readers go for recommendations. It's our priority at SFK Press to publish books for readers to enjoy, and our authors appreciate and value your feedback.

Our Southern Fried Guarantee

If you wouldn't enthusiastically recommend one of our books with a 4- or 5-star rating to a friend, then the next story is on us. We believe that much in the stories we're telling. Simply email us at *pr@sfkmultimedia.com*.

The Parlor Girl's Guide

Steve McCondichie

SFK
PRESS

SFK
PRESS

Published by
Southern Fried Karma, LLC
Atlanta, GA
www.sfkpress.com

Books are available in quantity for promotional or premium use. For
information, email pr@sfkmultimedia.com.

ISBN: 978-1-970137-99-6
eISBN: 978-1-970137-90-3
Library of Congress Control Number: 2019900031

Cover design by Olivia M. Croom. Cover art: Art Nouveau illustration by
Alfons Mucha. Interior by April Ford.

Printed in the United States of America.

To My Family,

Past, Present, and Future,

Given and Acquired.

Preface

My father's family was from Scots Station, Alabama, in the southern central part of the state. Scots Station was a real place, but, like my grandparents, it's gone. Not even a dot on the map. The town I created exists only in my mind, the same as the memories of my grandmother reciting stories on her front porch, my cousins, my sisters and I all huddled around her. If you'd like to hear more about Scots Station or other topics related to Molly's journey, connect to links at the end of select chapters throughout the novel.

Chapter 1

Thanksgiving 1926, Scots Station, Alabama

Molly Lingo awoke from her angel nightmare to the sound of her father singing "Jesus Loves Me," her favorite church hymn.

"Heaven's gates He's gonna open wide," he croaked, shaking her shoulder. He jerked down the threadbare blankets covering the family's front room window. The late autumn dawn bled into the room. "He will wash away my sin, And let all his sleepy headed childrens come on in."

Molly felt cold dampness on her back. The foul odor of her little brother's urine, like soggy hay, made the first inkling of sunlight seem harsher. The smell nudged her head away from her stubborn dream.

"Don't expect Stanley will ever learn to use the chamber pot or piss off the porch like his pap." Her father folded the blankets into wadded squares and stacked them in the washtub.

Stifling a yawn, Molly knew she needed to get out of bed and strip off her gown, but what she really wanted to do was slap her mother right across her floozy face. Tell her she was a no-account trollop for having an ill-begotten baby, thus obligating Molly to share her pallet and take care of him. Molly knew that folks in Scots Station looked at her with pity and shame whenever they saw her toting Stanley on her hip, assuming that she was as loose as her mother and raising some peckerwood's bastard child; with Alma Mae Lingo as her mother, no one would believe she was a virgin.

"Baby brother will crawl in with his momma," her father said. "If she'll let him."

Molly bent over and kissed Stanley's plump cheek. She'd never have the heart to push her three-year-old brother off their contorted cotton mattress onto the grungy plank floor, which stood only a couple of feet above the palmetto bugs and spiders that lurked underneath their shack.

"A grandson of a genuine Johnny Reb ought not to be hunting a Thanksgiving turkey," he said with a high-low pitch of joy and dread. "Damn carpetbagger holiday."

"You remember what Mr. Hinton said about hunting on his land?" Molly coerced her feet onto the floor.

"Zachary Hinton can kiss my narrow behind." Her father trudged into the kitchen.

As Molly rinsed her face in the leftover water in the basin bowl, last night's dream shoved its way back into her thinking. The three angels always appeared in her father's off-kilter plots like remnants of cloth blown together by the breeze. Shining like ruffled emeralds, the dark green tobacco leaves were broad and waxy. The field was next to the peeling school-house, withered vines clinging to the clapboards, or tucked between the town folk's church and the red brick grocery store. The angels stood tall and wide, towering over her father in their white linen suits, their faces clean shaven and pale as china clay, making their rosy cheeks glow unlike the tanned, scraggly look of her father. As she pulled off her soiled night-gown, she recalled one of the angels clutching her wrist. His soft hands were coarse against her skin, and she smiled at him with her eyes fixed on his heart.

The cold and the vision quickened her change into the long johns, flannel shirt, and dungarees she had laid out for their hunt. Her father clanging on the coffee pot pulled her thoughts back to the duties of the morning. She tucked her dark brown ponytail under a bandana wrapped around her head and pulled one of her father's tattered felt hats over the top. From across a wooded field, Hinton's overseer would believe a dad and his son were going on a hunt. Although the field boss had come around to check on Alma Mae and the baby four or five days after Stanley had been born, worrying that her father had ventured off on a bender the night after the midwife had left, leaving the Lingo plot unattended at the peak days for planting cotton seed. Still, her hunting outfit might fool him good enough until her father could snag a holiday turkey.

Her father's spite for Thanksgiving—like his first name, Skillet—came from his grandmother. After both his parents drowned crossing the Etowah River during a flood, her father came to his grandparents with only two possessions: a brass locket with a rhinestone quarter-moon on it, and a cast iron skillet. Great-Grandpa Lingo had lost his right arm at the Battle of Kennesaw Mountain, and Molly had heard her great-Granny Lingo's opinion of Thanksgiving, carpetbaggers, and John Wilkes Booth before. The Lingo family cherished their feuds.

Molly sat down for a small breakfast of thick coffee and her father's week-old buttermilk biscuits, noticing their dried-up gold and white edges. She stretched like a barn cat, arching from side to side. Molly believed her father had decided to ignore Lingo family tradition and Zachary Hinton's warning not to trespass on his turpentine plantation again, not because he felt blessed to be a hand-to-mouth tenant farmer and a clumsy thief, but because her father was afraid of Alma Mae—she was mean.

Her mother wasn't awake, but she had made it clear the night before that she wanted "the widest-rump turkey in the county" to put on her table, and not any "slimy squirrel meat or bony quail breasts" that they could have hunted on their own tenant farm. Some of her father's fear of Alma Mae had to do with her size. He was a slight man, shorter than Molly, and Alma Mae was a full-figured woman with muscular arms from hand-washing loads and loads of clothes all over Perry County. But most of his trepidation was because he tended to have a mild disposition—he had only ever threatened to beat the children or the mules.

Lacing up her black leather work boots, Molly tasted the backlash of her father's coffee. She walked out the shack's back door, slamming it behind her.

"Don't be so god-awful loud as to wake a legion of demons," he said, handing Molly the lead to Stonewall, their swayback mule. "You're cut from the same bolt of fine cloth that's for certain."

Molly snatched the rope and strode on, following her father. She didn't want to ruin their morning trip through the woods by snapping at him. Molly couldn't comprehend why when Stanley frayed Alma Mae's nerves, he would fix her a compress for her headache and take Stanley out to the porch, even though her little brother didn't resemble her father in the least bit. Molly guessed it was because her father was torn between fear of Alma Mae's wrath and bedevilment with Alma Mae's curves; she'd seen men admire her momma's rounded hips. On one of the rare afternoons when Molly was naked and alone in front of her mother's mirror, she had frowned when she noticed she'd developed the same showy buttocks that couldn't be covered with a secondhand calico dress. Molly was at least grateful that her eyes were speckled brown like pecan shells. If it weren't for the scar from Alma Mae's leather strap, her small lips would be lost below the jut of her nose. Her father said her oval face reminded him of a baby screech owl.

Guiding Stonewall through the untraceable path they took to reach the Hintons' land, Molly relished how the longleaf pines stood out against the vibrant oranges and reds of the changing hardwood trees.

"You doing OK, baby girl?" her father asked, leading her alongside a shallow creek.

"How far we going?" Molly replied.

"Far enough," her father said. "Try fancying yourself as the Pharaoh's daughter riding a cotton ball cloud across the grand blue sky to Beulah Land."

"I don't think they ride any clouds in the Bible."

"One old book ain't told everything God can do. Listen with more than your ears and look with more than your eyes."

"I know that don't happen in the Bible."

"Sure it does. You ain't reading it right."

As they continued on, Molly focused on the murmur of the creek and the thick succession of evergreens. In the woods, where she could smell the damp earth and hear it squish beneath her footsteps, it was easier to understand God than it was in Sunday school with some greasy-headed boy trying to squeeze her like she was a milk cow's teat every time Mr. Conyers, the high-pitched and half-witted deacon, turned his back. Out here, she sensed the pulsing of the ferns and the forest rolling in an enduring ripple, beyond where she could fathom.

They journeyed past their fallow fields, down and back up the steep bank heading into the marsh, and across a rutted farm-to-market road that was the borderline between their farm and Hinton's plantation.

After they tied Stonewall to a tree, they marched through a stretch of scraggly pine trees and wiregrass to a clearing on the interior of the Hinton plantation, far from the boundary road and their leased land. It was past midday when they tucked themselves behind a fallen oak tree. Waiting for an unsuspecting wild turkey to cross their path, her father planned their evening feast, talking on about fresh collards and black-eyed peas with ham hocks. The more swigs he took from the jug, the grander the meal became, adding rhubarb pies and caramel cakes.

"Then, after we're all fat and happy," her father said. "I'll get out my harmonica, and you and your momma can dance a jig with your baby brother."

"I don't know about all that," Molly said, squirming off a hard patch of ground.

"Sure, it'll be a swell old time like a family is supposed to do."

"First of all, we ain't killed no turkey. Second, you think Alma Mae is out of bed yet on her day off?"

"Damn, girl, here I am feeling a touch maudlin and you're acting all crotchety."

"Sorry, I'm just saying."

"I'm just saying we ain't like the town families, like Hinton, who probably already ate his wide-rump bird, then patted his wife and kids on the noggin like little dogs, and ran off with the boys to his hunting camp to tell his pack of lies."

Her father took a long pull from his jug and handed the corn liquor to Molly. She accepted his offer, sipping it, hoping to ease the knots of worry looping around her temples. The angels from her nightmare kept appearing in snippets. Bleached cheeks and honeyed voices, and a glint of flames in the tallest one's eyes. His heart, visible through his linen suit, was as black as swamp water and pumped a rotten sludge. The young woman with long flowing brown hair, who'd always been in her dreams, was shouting and crisscrossing through the rows of tobacco plants, and with each stride, she was farther away. The black-hearted angel stroked Molly's thigh. She strained to heed the woman's warning, but her legs were fence posts jammed into the ground. There was no breaking away in either world. Those rare moments when her father wasn't drunk or desperate to be drunk, he'd inquire about her nightly dreams, claimed his grandmother always asked if any were clearer than the rest, brighter, but Alma Mae had no use for idle talk that kept you from scrubbing out her piss pot.

Only the shrill gobbling from a gang of wild turkeys approaching through the wiregrass chased the images away.

"You hear that? Sounds like we got us some dinner coming our way," her father said. He'd made little effort all afternoon to attract any prey with his homemade turkey call, a small piece of slate and a deer bone. They were fortunate that any birds were moving at all this close to dusk.

"Shhhh," Molly said, holding her index finger to her lips.

"Hand me Reliable," he whispered, having put Molly in charge of the shotgun so he could reach his corn liquor and tobacco whenever he needed, which was often. The Parker double-barrel shotgun was the Lingo family jewel. Molly had heard two different versions of the gun's origin. The gun had either been handed down by great-Granny Lingo as a wedding present or her father had stolen it in self-defense from his new father-in-law the night he and Alma Mae eloped. Either way, it was the family's main source of meat.

Five gray hens and two gobblers appeared through an opening in the grass, bobbing their necks with each step. Molly handed her father the shotgun. The hens strutted around the gobblers, who were trilling back and forth as they paraded side-by-side with their white and black tail feathers fanning out.

"Look at the beard on that tomboy," he said, raising his shotgun, the barrel wobbling as he tried to keep it steady. "That'll make Alma Mae dance me an Irish jig."

As the gang got closer, Molly could see the trail of copper and gold feathers in the center of the lead male's chest. She saw her father's crooked index finger on the trigger, and she closed her eyes and covered her ears.

The blast of the Parker shook her, and Molly heard the quavering chorus of the turkeys. When she opened her eyes, she expected to see a dead turkey on the ground.

"Hellfire, damn gun," he said, the birds all flying a few feet up in the air and scrambling back down. He let loose the second barrel of the shotgun, and again the turkeys fluttered and then scattered along the edge of the grass, their cries filling the woods.

Her father cracked open the shotgun and dug in his coat pocket for one last shell. He jammed the shell into the barrel and snapped the barrel shut. Molly would have as soon watched her momma choke on the wishbone than dance a jig, but she still said *please Jesus* to herself.

An instant after the crack of the gun, the smaller of the two males dropped to the ground, thrashing in circles.

"We got us a jake, baby girl," he said, stumbling back onto the fallen oak tree. "Go get 'em."

"You want *me* to go get him?" Molly said, pressing her back to the tree trunk.

"I did the killing—you do the fetching."

Molly didn't budge; her job was to keep her father company, not retrieve dying wild turkeys.

"Go on, girl. Skinflint Hinton might've heard those shots. I'll meet you where we got Stonewall tied up. Run on." Her father staggered towards the woods with the Parker slung over his shoulder.

The surviving male bird began to peck at the smaller one's eyes. The dying bird let out a weak, throaty sound.

"Stop that now. You mean old bastard," Molly shouted, running toward the downed turkey. She grabbed a stick and threw it at the merciless survivor. "Get on out of here."

The gobbler gave one last poke to the vanquished turkey before it pursued the hens marching back into the wiregrass, leaving Molly alone with her family's flailing Thanksgiving dinner. She watched it fight to breathe. The ground around it was scattered with feathers. If Skillet had made a clean head-shot, her job fetching the turkey would have been simpler, but he had been too drunk and hit the bird's mid-section. Death would be slow unless she helped. The sunlight was growing dimmer, and she was worried that she'd have to lug the turkey through the dark woods, battling coyotes and foxes, to get dinner home safely. The bird thrashed about when she moved in closer. She walked around the struggling turkey and spotted a stone as large as a loaf of bread; she picked it up and cradled it between her legs as she waddled over to the bird, who stared up at her, its mangled eye blinking. The instant before she dropped the rock on its head, Molly swore the dying jake pleaded for mercy. Any other last sounds the bird might have made were muted by the thud of the stone on its skull.

Molly rolled the stone away and hoisted the wild turkey over her shoulder. Heading to meet her father, she squeezed the matted feathers, her palms warm and moist with innards and goop. When she got home, she was going to plop their loot down on the front porch and tell Alma Mae to get her lazy rump plucking and skinning.

Want to learn about the role of Scots Station in Lingo family life? Subscribe to Southern Fried Karma's YouTube channel, Fugitive Views.

Chapter 2

Ready to drop her burden, Molly weaved through the slicing wiregrass and the thin skeletal trees that jutted up from the ground. The sun plummeted below the horizon, transforming the forest light from silver to dark gray. She'd kiss Stonewall when she saw him.

"Psst, baby girl . . . Psst . . . over here."

Molly halted and shifted her load, resisting the weight of the lifeless bird and the lukewarm blood trickling down the back of her dungarees.

"Help my narrow b-b-bee-hind up," her father said in the disembodied voice of a drunken phantom. He stuttered when he was drunkest, or when he was dodging Alma Mae's leather strap.

She scanned the woods for her father. A murky curtain enclosed the forest around her. "Help you up? Where you at?"

"Help me up, or I'll just stay f-f-falling out."

Following the sound of her father's voice, Molly spotted a shadowy lump on the ground propped against a tree. She moved closer, leaning down to be sure it wasn't a nighttime trick of the woods. The hot sting of corn liquor rose up from the figure. Molly slung the jake to the ground and reached out for her father to hoist him up.

"Not so fast." Lurching up, he rocked back and forth, steadying himself against the tree trunk. "That's better." He pulled his jacket tight around his neck. "Alrighty then, I'll carry my wide-rump prize home to Alma Mae. You lead Stonewall." He jerked in the direction of the bushes shielding the mule.

"Why don't I strap it across the top and you lead him?"

"Cause I've been b-busy," he said, staggering over to untie the mule.

As her father fought against himself to push and pull Stonewall out of hiding, Molly could hear the jangling of the load. The family mule was carrying enough corn liquor jugs to fill half a wagon. The butt of Reliable stuck out in the air.

"What in the world did you do?" Molly asked, wishing she didn't have to ask or hear her father's reply.

"I ran by Hinton's copper pot still and picked me up a few jugs on credit."

Molly peered at the mangled turkey she had lugged from the field and then yanked the lead line from her father's hand to guide Stonewall.

"Ouch, sourpuss, let's get you a piece of p-p-peppermint or some taffy to sweeten you up." He hoisted the dead bird onto his shoulder.

"If there's any sweets back in that cabin, Alma Mae fed them to Stanley."

"Damn, girl, m-misery is optional," her father said, turning his back and beginning their march home.

Shortly, they were at the hedgerow before the boundary road, and her father stopped to catch his breath. "Loose me that half-empty jug."

Molly remained stock-still

"It's the one there on the end."

Standing stiff, Molly stared at the moon rising above the tops of the trees.

"Come on, toting our dinner is doing me in."

"Can't untie it here in the dark without the risk of breaking them," Molly said, the load tightening her back and legs.

"You are a hard woman," he said with a dull laugh. "Let me check the road." He disappeared between the hedges and reappeared. "We'll be home lickety-split. Hurry every time you think about it."

Molly stepped through the hedgerow, tugging Stonewall along. Both directions of the road were dark corridors. Venus flickered above the yellow crescent moon, veiled by low-hanging clouds. The hushed evening air should've been peaceful, but Molly could hear the loud jangling of the jugs as they crossed the boundary road. She winced and silently said *thank you, Jesus for providing us with this smashed jake and stolen hooch and please protect me from any black-hearted angels and Alma Mae. And please allow Stanley to not piss the bed tonight.*

They descended into the marsh, and with each plodding step water soaked through her boots. As they hiked up the embankment, leaving the marsh and Hinton's land behind, the thud of horse hooves and men yelling edged into the woods. Spotting the glow of torches bobbing through the night, Molly tightened her grip on the mule's rope and scurried up the bank alongside her father. The two rushed across the rows of their tilled-up field.

"Over yonder," a man's voice boomed, trailing them from the top of the embankment.

The thick gumbo dirt clutched at her wet boots, stymieing each step.

The blows of their hooves grew heavier as the horsemen pounded over the field and encircled them as they all reached the end of the field. Her father flung the dead jake to the ground and pulled Reliable from Stonewall's pack. Dazed, Molly tried to focus on the posse surrounding them. The glow of the torches illuminated five riders with burlap seed bags covering their faces, Zach Hinton at the head on a gray stallion.

"Whoa," Hinton shouted, reining in his mount.

Her father spun around, pointing the family shotgun at all the riders. The heaving puffs of the lathered horses pushed them in close, surrounding them.

"God damn, Whip, knock that shotgun out of that fool's hands before he blasts someone," one of the men squawked.

Molly recognized the high-pitched belonging to Mr. Conyers, her Sunday school teacher. The man next to him was so short his feet didn't hang but halfway down his horse's barrel. That had to be Pug O'Neal, Hinton's brother-in-law and the mayor of Scots Station. One of the other masked men pulled a bullwhip from his saddle, and Molly knew that was Whip Bannister, Hinton's overseer, whose family had been flogging Perry County field hands for generations.

Hinton held his hand up. "Take it easy, Deacon. Whip and I know how to handle this. Besides, we aim to talk first."

"What you want talk about, Mr. Zach? Ask me how my Thanksgiving has been?" her father pointed his shotgun square at Whip's chest. "Tell you the truth, I don't shine much to carpet-bagger holidays."

"Now Skillet, ease your old gun down off my man," Hinton said in a deep, round voice like he was blessing a family dinner. He leaned forward in his saddle, a live oak looming above them.

"I kinda like it right where it's at for now."

"Sure, I understand. But you mind if I ask where you shot that turkey you're toting?"

"Bagged it in the marsh bottom, right past my fields."

"So you're saying that wasn't your three shots we heard on my land right before sunset?"

"Must've been the wind playing tricks with the sounds."

"Same kind of trick that raided ten jugs of my homebrew?"

"We can talk about that," her father said, moving closer to Molly.

Hinton shook his head and slid off his stallion. He was wearing his ash gray Sunday suit, but the collar was undone, and the tie was twisted loose. His unbuttoned pinstripe vest flapped about. "Might be past talking on that subject." He approached Molly, inspecting her up and down. "I didn't think that bastard boy living with you was old enough to be out hunting, but this ain't no schoolboy. Is it?"

"Mr. Hinton, I gotta tell you, my momma is most likely terrible worried about where we're at," Molly said, the bile boiling in her stomach. "I'm sure she went to town to fetch the sheriff."

"Fetch the sheriff?" Hinton yelled to the men behind him. They all laughed aloud. "Sweet-cakes, if Alma Mae came upon that knee-walking drunk bastard this evening, it'd be so he'd crack her open like your pappy's rusty little shotgun."

"Ain't no need for all that vile talk, Mr. Zach," her father said, moving closer to Hinton, blocking his path to Molly with the barrel of the shotgun.

"You still owe me ninety-five dollars from this fall's crop." Hinton's tone was as sharp as a honed sickle. "I heard tales about you selling a portion of your yield before the auction, so I wouldn't get all mine. You cut me out."

"This spring is gonna be a real b-b-bounty, and all we got to do is work that out, like businessmen d-d-do," her father said.

Molly noticed her father's trembling chin, and his panic passed into her chest.

"*D-d-do* what, you stuttering fool? You want to work that out tonight? Right here and now?"

"Maybe we could work it out for a piece of Alma Mae's cooch," Conyers said with a delighted shriek. "It's been a while since she's been out to the Sporting Lodge."

"Even Pug has had too many pieces of that pie. I got a tastier tart in my mind," Hinton grabbed for Molly, like she was a loose hen running in the yard.

The soreness from the long day's task tingled throughout her limbs.

"Whoa, that's enough," her father said, smacking Hinton flush across the face with the shotgun.

Hinton pulled his hand back to cover his nose. Howling, blood seeping between his fingers, he bent over, sticking his head between his knees.

Her father aimed a squinted eye at Molly. A jittery string of muscle spasms quaked from her thigh around to her butt. Alma Mae and her leather strap would be a satisfying sight now.

"Hellfire, Zachary, you're bleeding like a speared sow," Pug O'Neal said, bursting out in a dimwitted snicker. "How you gonna explain that to my big sister?"

Hinton retched out a mouthful of grisly spit, and he wiped his bloody hand on his vest. "You no-account broke dick." He wrenched the shotgun out of her father's hands and swung the butt across her father's head, knocking him to the ground, and then he jammed the tip of the gun into Skillet's groin and pulled the trigger.

Click-click.

"You pointed a damn empty gun at me?" Hinton screamed.

Molly lunged at her father's maddened attacker, clawing at his face, but three or four searing cracks from Whip's cat o' nine tails tore through her flimsy jacket and sent her reeling into the black dirt. From there, Molly watched Hinton raise Reliable high above his head, forming an inverted wishbone with the shotgun and his massive arms. Hinton hammered the traitorous gun down onto her father, and, catching her look, planted the spurred heel of his riding boot across her shoulders. Once more he drove the butt of the shotgun down on Skillet, bashing the weapon across his neck and head, and once more Molly struggled to rescue her fallen father. Hinton buried her face into the ground with his boot and smashed her father two, three, four times or more, the sounds morphing from brittle cracks to wet thuds. Each satisfied grunt from Hinton was met by withering groans from Skillet.

The bleak taste of the damp earth forged a path into her mouth, but she swallowed it. Managing somehow to roll away, she saw the butchered purplish-red butt of the gun and Hinton's sneer shimmering in the marigold torchlight. Hinton tossed the shotgun aside, and two of the masked men stepped around her, working with a split rail and a stretch of rope, while the others howled, "Hellfire," "son-of-a-bitch," and "two-bit whore." She strained to stand, to find Reliable; the family shotgun was proof of what they'd done, and she had to know how, her father was, what was happening to him now. Raising herself on all fours, Molly saw her father being dragged away—through his own field—his screams blending with the posse's yells and fading.

Chapter 3

The first drops of pelting rain awoke Molly, who was coiled up in the dirt. The moon was buried by storm clouds, and night covered the field. Molly grimaced at the pain burning across her shoulder blades as she uncurled. She felt for her tattered, blood-soaked jacket and thought of Stanley and Alma Mae. Her mother would understand what had happened and why. She would give Molly answers that her father couldn't. She staggered backward, as though still carrying the weight of the dead jake, but the wide-rump prize and Stonewall were nowhere to be seen. Lowering her head against the rainfall, she started toward the creek.

By the time she reached the bank, the rain was a steady downpour, and the rolling waters created a rumbling stream. Molly wriggled along a fallen oak above the stream, and as she made it to the other side, Stonewall came forward, bowing his head to greet her. She ran her hand along his damp mane, stroking his neck. His swayback was bare: no pack, no stolen jugs, no dead jake. She was foolish for having expected Hinton to exchange a beating for his corn liquor and his turkey; he was a taker, not a trader. Alma Mae should've known better than to allow them to be put in that situation. Leading the mule to his lean-to shed, she undid his harness and poured the last of the grain into his feedbag. Stonewall was the only member of the family to witness what had happened to her father. Rubbing him down before heading inside, Molly recalled reading to her father and little brother the Doctor Doolittle tales, and how Skillet claimed the power to talk to the animals. Her stomach twisted, tight and hard, and she half-retched, resisting the impulse to vomit.

The back door to their cabin was unlatched. Molly paused

on the porch and considered removing her waterlogged boots, but she stepped into the kitchen without further concern for the results. The dying embers still burned in the potbelly stove and two plates sat on the stovetop, covered in napkins. The strength drained from her chest, down her stomach, and poured out her legs. The room whirled around her and her knees trembled.

Alma Mae shuffled into the kitchen, holding out her bedside lamp.

Molly battled to manage her balance.

"I better not find you hauling mud into the house I've been cleaning all day," Alma Mae said. "Where's your daddy at? I ought to take the strap to both of you."

Molly stared at her mother—her face swollen from sleep, her open robe exposing her drooping tits—then turned away.

"Stanley and me made tinkle in the outhouse and killed us a few squirrels with some red devils and a slingshot." Alma Mae sat the oil lamp down, tightened her faded flannel robe, and moved toward the stove. "I fixed us a Brunswick stew, baby brother threw in a few acorns. We baked some of my momma's crackling bread. Burnt my damn pumpkin pie worrying about you two. Go on and sit down. You can clean up after you eat a bit. Don't expect Skillet fed you much today."

Molly put her hands on the back of the cane chair, allowing it to carry her burden.

"Take your load off, baby girl. Nobody is gonna get walloped on a holiday. I'll serve you a plate, no need to wait 'til your daddy comes inside." Alma Mae set a plate on the table and pulled the stained linen napkin off the plate. Miss Jewell, a shriveled hag from town and one of her regular laundry customers, had given the napkins to Alma Mae, and neither apple cider vinegar nor scrubbing could remove the ruby spots.

"I don't think he'll be home tonight," Molly said.

"He might be howling-at-the-moon drunk, but Skillet

always comes home to me."

Molly twisted her back to her mother, showing her the lashes.

"What in tarnation?" Alma Mae eased the jacket off Molly's back and unbuttoned her overalls. "I told Skillet to watch for those bastards, secret society of drunken bullies. How bad a beating they give your daddy? Let me fetch the washbasin out of my room."

Molly sat down at that table and buried her face in her hands. When she looked up, her mother was peeling off her torn flannel shirt.

"Where's your daddy at?" her mother said, dabbing Molly's wounds.

Between her muzzled cries and her mother scolding her to sit still, Molly recounted the events of the day, struggling to fit the scrambled pieces together. "Before Hinton went all crazy, I told them that you were fetching the sheriff."

Alma Mae pulled away from Molly's back and soaked her washrag in the basin. "These cuts need iodine before I bandage 'em. You want a fix for the pain?"

"Where do you think they took Skillet?" Molly said, turning to face her mother straight on.

"You heard your daddy screaming, didn't ya'?" Alma Mae stepped away, pulling two bottles out of the cupboard. "Could ya' tell if he was—"

Molly fixed a disgusted glare on her mother.

"They probably hauled him to the city lockup for the weekend. He ain't the first busted-ass sharecropper in Scots Station to get run on a rail for stealing and owing money."

"You been to this Sporting Lodge before?" Molly formed a fist, ready to guard against an attack from her mother's thick brown strap.

"Don't you make the fool mistake of believing everything you here a man brag about. I work all over the county for all kinda folks. If I had to venture out to that hunting camp and clean and wash for some Daddy Warbucks visiting from Birmingham and Atlanta, well then, that's what I had to do for us to get by.

"You drink some of this. Then you eat if you can. You don't wanna feel no more tonight. If your Daddy ain't home by Sunday supper, I'll fetch the sheriff, sure enough, or go up to Hinton's house for an accounting. He can't earn keep for no one idling in the pokey. Now go on and take you a dose." Alma Mae set the smaller of the bottles in front of Molly.

"What is it?" Molly said, picking up the short half-full brown bottle.

"A numbing tonic."

Molly removed the cork stopper and sniffed the thick amber fluid. "Whew, that smells worse than Stanley's nasty diddy. What's in it?"

"A tincture of poppy and wormwood, mighty hard to come by, and it's sorta ripe smelling, but before too long you'll be grateful I shared it with you."

Molly raised the bottle to her lips and hesitated, thinking over the offer. Praying now that Alma Mae wouldn't poison her, accidentally or otherwise, seemed as foolish as believing that it was possible for honey to flow from a rock or a man to come back from the dead.

"Don't dwell on it, drink it," her mother ordered.

Molly tilted her head back and allowed the medicine to spill into her mouth. Silence was the better bargain for now. She'd deal with Jesus, Alma Mae, and Hinton later. She gagged as the bitter fluid slithered down her throat and into her belly, and soon a breezy wave lifted her away from thoughts of her father and Hinton.

"Ease up," her mother said, wresting the medicine bottle from Molly's hand. "That feels better, don't it?"

"It does." The strength that had flooded out earlier now washed back into her chest and rushed out the top of her skull. "Mm, it does," Molly hummed, resting her head on the table, the warmth caressing every aching muscle. She closed her eyes, opening herself up to dreams.

For two days, Alma Mae nursed her, giving up her bedroom and letting her sleep alone while she and Stanley stayed on her pallet in the front room. Alma Mae served her heaping bowls of vegetable soup mixed with cornbread, and gave her regular doses of numbing tonic, watered-down in a jar. It wasn't as powerful as the first fix, but it eased the pain of the healing lashes and allowed Molly to sleep most of the time. And for two days, she dreamt of searching for Skillet as the black-hearted angels chased her across rising creeks and endless marshes of knee-high sludge, the untamed stares of their stallions pressing on her back, bearing down, as she climbed winding swamp oaks and stormed through briar patches, calling out for her father. Only the occasional glimpse of the brown-haired woman from behind a dogwood tree gave Molly any peace. The woman's tender gaze had been a fixture of the earliest dreams she could recall—leading her to meadows of purple and golden wildflowers. There'd been one time, Molly was certain of it, when the young brown-haired woman had appeared in the room soon after Molly woke up after a tornado nightmare. She'd sat cross-legged next to her pallet. The scent of peppermint oil flowed through the family room as the hint of dawn broke through the curtains. Releasing a cloudy whisper in her ear, she told Molly, before her mother's belly had begun to swell, that soon she'd have a baby brother. That evening, Skillet let out on a weeklong bender and Alma Mae laid the leather strap across Molly's mouth.

On a dull gray Sunday afternoon, Molly woke up with Stanley squatting on the bed next to her, tapping her cheek with a frayed book.

"Read me," her little brother said.

Molly groaned.

"Read me." Stanley increased the intensity of his tapping and thrust the book onto his sister's chest.

Easing herself up in the bed, Molly peeled the quilt back, giving her brother room to slide in next to her. "OK, OK," she said, rubbing the sleep from her eyes and focusing on the book. "*Ragged Dick?*"

Stanley bounced up and down under the quilt.

"Big surprise." Molly had read Horatio Alger Jr.'s story of the young New York City bootblack to her brother at least a dozen times before, and they usually enjoyed Dick Hunter's adventures and never-ending cheer.

"I take me a catnap and you're up to the devil," her mother said, storming into the bedroom. "You need a tanning?"

Stanley ducked under the covers and squirmed out the side of the bed, crouching on the floor for a moment. Alma Mae went around the side of the bed, and Stanley darted under it.

"You snot-nosed rascal. See how long you can stay under there in the dark with all them creepy crawly bugs." Alma Mae peered down at Molly. "I warned him." She took the book and put the back of her hand on her forehead. "Don't seem like you're feverish. You want a dose before I get your supper?"

"You heard anything?"

"I'll be right back. Baby brother, I got your darling little book. So you best come on before I toss it in the fire." Alma Mae left the bedroom, and Stanley crawled out from under the bed and chased after her. Within moments, Molly heard the slaps of Alma Mae's hand striping her brother's fleshy thighs, followed by his piercing squalls. He was still bawling in the front room when Alma Mae came in with the medicine.

"Drink this to tolerate that whining," her mother said, handing the jar to Molly.

"Are you going to fetch the sheriff?"

"Not much left, so I had to cut this dose down some more."

"You said there'd be an accounting," Molly said, risking a huffy tone and the strap, or whatever else her mother could take hold of to deliver a lick.

"As likely as not your daddy is high and dry in the pokey," Alma Mae crossed her arms along the front of her long, yellowish-brown housedress. A muslin sugar sack would've been more flattering. "I ain't tromping to town in the rain and cold. Take your dose."

Molly inspected the dingy jam jar. Most town ladies in Scots Station used them for canning preserves, hand-picking wild blackberries, or harvesting fresh green beans and cucumbers from their own vegetable gardens. They'd spend hours sweating over boiling pots in their steaming late-summer kitchens, setting up shelves in their pantries, and filling them with supplies for the family to enjoy the rest of the year. But Molly didn't need a sweet, navy-blue spread to make her morning pastry tastier, she wanted a return to her slumber. "Where's this potion came from? Doc K or the pharmacy?" Molly downed a third of the jar.

"You ain't gonna wanna know."

"Where from?" Molly asked before she finished the medicine.

"Like I said."

"Tell me."

"Near Scots Station there ain't but one place," her mother said, sharing a secret family recipe. "So I trek my weary ass out to the Sporting Lodge to horse trade with that haughty hussy that runs the house for Mr. Zach. That painted-up New Orleans cunny owns more silk corsets than some gals have teeth, all lined up her in closet. Looks like a Jezebel rainbow." Alma Mae laughed aloud.

"I'll read to Stanley," Molly said, smiling. "Usually calms him down."

"Eat you a bite before you doze off again. I'll handle baby—" Alma Mae cut herself short when she heard the chugging of an automobile engine. The low growl stopped in front of their cabin. Next, there was the metallic banging of car doors followed by boots on the front porch and a bang on the front door.

Stanley ran into the room and grabbed hold of his mother's legs.

"Alma Mae, open up," the voice from the porch ordered.

Despite her groggy state, Molly recognized Zach Hinton's puffed-up tone.

"Who is it?" Alma Mae lifted Stanley up and put him on the bed with Molly.

"Charlie Chaplin and Buster Keaton."

"Mr. Zach?" she replied, clasping her arms across her breasts.

"Come on now, it's blustering out here."

"Just a second." Alma Mae turned to her children and raised her index finger to her lips. "Shhh." She shut the bedroom door behind her.

Loud voices filtered under the door. Molly's little brother burrowed himself under the covers, while she wobbled over to the door and cracked it open. Zach Hinton and Whip Bannister stood in the middle of their front room, each man dressed in his dark church suit.

"I wanna know. Did you take Skillet out to the pit?" Alma Mae asked, wiping beads of sweat from her forehead.

"You best forget what you're presuming about the pit. Those other fellows are incorrigible and got carried away is all." Hinton trod closer to Alma Mae. "I warned him. We talked about his predicament."

"You never said anything about—what did you boys do with my husband?"

"He left town on his own accord."

"Left town?"

"That's right, quit his lease, and gave up on me, and you, owing money that someone has got to pay."

"That ain't right." Alma Mae paced back and forth in the front room. "No way."

"Me and you both know, he was prone to dereliction. Hellfire, the whole county knows. I estimate he sodded off like a boozy tramp, hopped a train. But being your family name is on the lease, that makes you responsible for the debt. Three-hundred-seventy-five is my fairest calculation."

Alma Mae stopped and glared at the two men in her front room.

The hammering of Molly's heart resonated throughout her body.

Hinton leaned in closer and lowered his voice. "By all accounts of Alabama law, I got sufficient reason to stand before Judge Finley and have him declare a default judgment and sign eviction papers. But I aim to settle, so you aren't doing laundry for the county prisoners while those two children of yours get placed in the Presbyterian home over in Talladega. Ms. Lynn says it's not too awful a place. But you don't want some deviant shopkeeper hauling your daughter off or some factory boss working your baby boy's fingers 'til they're bloody nubs."

"I've heard enough kitchen gossip and washed enough of Ms. Lynn's linens to wonder how she'd feel about what went on the other night," Alma Mae said, her voice hardening against Hinton's threats.

"Don't think you possess any poker chips to play at my table," Hinton said, shaking his head. He spat a stream of brown tobacco juice onto the floor. "I got a bargain for you, but I ain't tolerating no sass mouth."

"You can stick your bargain right up Ms. Lynn's bunghole."

Hinton grabbed Alma Mae's cheeks and squeezed them tight. "You white trash whore."

Heat flushed through her throat. Molly grabbed the jam jar, and swinging the bedroom open wide, hurled it at Hinton's head. The glass smashed on the wall behind him. Whip grabbed Molly and flung her down on her pallet. Hinton shoved Alma Mae down on the floor next to Molly, and Stanley scurried out to join his mother and sister, huddling close.

"Damn it all, if she ain't as spunky as her momma. Got more gumption than her pappy," Hinton said with a coarse laugh.

Alma Mae pulled Stanley and Molly in closer. Stanley buried his face in Molly's neck. His runny nose was soft and warm. Molly wrapped her arm around her mother's waist, pressing her fingers into Alma Mae's side.

"I'm gonna give you a choice." Hinton planted his feet in front of them, broadening his stance. "One of you two is coming with me to work off your debt out at the Sporting Lodge, and the other can mind the baby."

"Mr. Zach, I'm sorry." Alma Mae let go of her children and knelt in front Hinton like a sinner at the foot of the cross.

"I'd say one full season, from the big buck rut to bass fishing, is all it'd take to make me whole. Cleaning, washing, a little sporting. That is unless you got three-hundred-seventy-five hidden up your bunghole?"

"Please," Alma Mae moaned, rubbing Hinton's pants leg.

"Everyone in Perry County knows I'm owed a bona fide obligation." Hinton slapped her hand away. "One of you two is coming with me, and the other is clearing out in the morning."

Shivers swept over Molly, and the last dose of numbing tonic fogged her mind. She wanted them all to leave so Stanley and she could curl up for a rest. When they woke up, she'd read him his story, and *Ragged Dick*—not Jesus—would show them how to overcome their misfortunes.

Raising herself up, Alma turned around and grabbed the side of her daughter's face, exhaling. "It'll only be house chores, not nothing else. I'll go to Moab Mountain, up north of Florence. Get the money from my momma and daddy." She shut her eyes and pulled Molly near, resting her chin on the crown of her skull. "I swear it won't be no time."

"That settles it then," Hinton said with a grin like he'd

struck a deal to buy a prized sow.

Whip reached down and lifted a woozy Molly up, using his thick forearm to secure his load. The tonic's trance melted her resistance, enabling her to dream that all this unpleasantness was only temporary—a cloudy memory the moment it occurred.

Alma Mae hurried into the bedroom and came scampering out the door as Whip walked off the porch, toting Molly across his shoulder "Take this." She forced a bag into her daughter's dangling hand, but Molly lost her weak grip on it as soon as Whip bound over a puddle towards Hinton's automobile.

The overseer lowered Molly into the back seat of Hinton's sky blue sedan.

"Bannister, you owe me to do right by her," her mother said, carrying a wailing and kicking Stanley out to the front yard, her arms folded over her son's.

Retrieving the small bag from the mud puddle, Whip stuck the soggy purple velveteen pouch in his jacket pocket. The loud knocking of the Chrysler's engine drowned out her brother's high-pitched cries as Molly rode off with Alma Mae racing beside the car for as long as she could stand.

Discover more about abuses of tenant farming in the rural South by subscribing to Southern Fried Karma's YouTube channel, Fugitive Views.

Chapter 4

Up until tonight, Thanksgiving was Cotton Arnold's favorite holiday. He didn't have to suffer marching in the out-of-step Independence Day parades. There was no fussing with parties crammed with caramel cakes and sausage balls. No opening bootlicking Christmas gifts addressed to Mr. & Mrs. Arnold and Cornelius. Thanksgiving should have been a pleasant meal with relatives. He wasn't the instigator that ruined the evening. His cousin's fiancée had been the rabble-rouser, and Lucius Arnold, his father, had seen her adjusting the strap on her snakeskin print dress when they'd walked back into the room. His piqued father would relish lambasting his mother with what he'd endured like he was a martyr at the Colosseum.

Thankfully, neither Cotton's young cousin, Will, nor his uncle, were as observant as Lucius. Cotton's Uncle Allan had provided him with a lift to Dwyer, and the darkie had dropped him at the square after his aunt and uncle passed out on the ride from the Arnold's family farm back into town. Cotton told Jeremiah a brisk stroll in the autumn air would serve him well.

The restless square was barren as if a plague had infested the city. In front of the west entrance to the towering courthouse, the U.D.C. had erected a statue as a memorial to those fallen for the Lost Cause. Dwyer's collection of crones must have believed the marble night watchman appeared courageous.

"Sorry, chum." Cotton released a stream of piss at the granite base of the courthouse memorial. If bravery meant risking a Minié ball to the brain for a plot of land he'd never profit from, then the stoic sentry carried all the courage he'd ever need. Infantrymen in the C.S.A. were fodder for the plantation elites, the same as 32-pounder solid shots, tobacco seed, and barefoot pickaninnies.

Cotton shook the last drops of urine off onto the cobblestone. He heard the mechanical click of the big hand reaching the top of the dial. A dozen strikes of the brass bell vibrated in his chest. Cotton hitched up his britches and headed towards home, venturing down the cobbled thoroughfare that the Scots-Irish settlers had used as a bumpy wagon road to the ferry, and which before that was a hunting trail forged by the Lower Creek Indians a thousand years before the birth of Christ.

Plodding past muted haberdasheries and dress shops, he steered his drunken thoughts to Louise's long legs, which belonged to a filly. She was more racehorse than young Will, a bookish lad, could handle. Cotton's cock started to get hard. Serendipity had placed the two coquettish hellions down the back hallway. The secluded passageway, lined with Dutch stilllifes, was fit for a dalliance. The red-headed provocateur apologized for interrupting his father while he was trying to remember a line from "Horatius at the Bridge," and thanked Cotton with a kiss for joining in her jumbled discussion of Dorothy Parker's poetry and the Fitzgeralds' latest scandal. After a night of vintage Bordeaux, slipping his hand under the beaded hem of her gown seemed like a bright idea, until the maid coughed and clanked her tray of dirty cups and saucers as she entered the hallway. Adah's darts and twitches conveyed enough for him to realize that Mr. Arnold had noticed the willful pair was missing.

A needle rain began as he tarried on the sidewalk in front of Dr. North's white-columned house on Jackson Street, the Greek revival mansion he'd aimlessly searched for in nightmares. Waiting on her parents' porch, the cluster of wicker furniture arranged in a tight rectangle, is where he'd always picture Mary Katherine, reading her *Diddie, Dumps & Tot* or thumbing through *McCall's*. When he offered M.K. a promise ring, the thin gold band, she'd moved from their cozy love-seat to the beige wicker chair nearer the steps as if she were cranking the handle on a flicker photo kit. How foolish it was to imagine her there tonight, too restless to sleep, stealing a smoke in the vacant loveseat. Cotton wanted no further visits to that sprawling porch or the brickwork sanitarium they'd led to.

Entering the foyer at home, the Arnolds' townhouse was empty, enveloped in shadows and silence. His parents would be out at the family farm all weekend, his mother perhaps longer. She found comfort in Creekside's drawing room and the portraits of a tow-headed Cotton and his older brother, Luke, still ripe with potential. Climbing the stairs to his bed-room, sensing solace in each creak of the steps, he squelched the vision of a uniformed servant girl delivering a breakfast tray. That was as preposterous as him expecting a lonesome Mary Katherine to be waiting on the Norths' porch.

Cotton kicked off his shoes, plopped down on his bed, and rolled over onto his back. The new electric light dangled from the ceiling, the pendant fixture hanging as easy as the wide straps draped across Louise's freckled shoulders. Her embroidered tan gown had slipped off and on as if it been had designed with the wistful hint of a quickie as a criterion. His erection returned. Of course, he wanted to fuck her, she was a vigorous new wine, but she needed a rescuer. He'd decant her liquid soul into his own and smuggle her out of Creekside's front door. They'd picnic in a cloistered meadow. Relishing the purloined wine that she'd once been, he'd hoist her long legs over his shoulders and screw her in the stark sunlight.

Yawning, he stretched out on his tidy double bed counting on a proper wank to put him to sleep. He had to get on the road early in the morning. As the only bachelor on the Tri-State Supply sales staff it was his duty to chaperone a group of procurement agents and lumber yard managers on a trip to a hunting lodge in Alabama, some backwoods bordello south of

Montgomery. On the way out of Dwyer, he stopped at Huck's for fried eggs, a half-dozen slices of thick peppered bacon, and a few bottles of his friend's moonshine. As long as it had stopped raining, he put the top down on his gold La Salle and drink his blue fame shine. Will and Louise's wedding in April would be an awkward outing. By next Thanksgiving, she should be pimply and pregnant, and he should have caught his own flirtatious fiancée to irritate his father. A weekend of whores and whiskey was more than rife with sufficient potential to let him forget Lucius Arnold's glare and the Norths' vacant porch.

Chapter 5

Slumped over in the back seat, Molly worked to notice where they were going. At least three or four times a year, she'd ridden on the Perry County school bus, and the Pentecostal Holiness Church bus picked her up every week at the end of the road for Sunday school and worship service, but this was the first time she'd ever been in a passenger car. The columns of pine trees ticked past as they traveled down the scrawny dirt lane she'd only ever walked before. At the end of the farm-to-market road, she'd always turned right to go to town, but instead Whip turned left and accelerated onto the paved state highway. The only sights familiar to Molly now were the patches of cotton fields, a few downy wisps still stuck to the ragged stalks.

"Straight to the old mill cottage?" Whip asked.

"Nope, direct to the Lodge," Hinton said, rolling down the window and spitting out his tobacco plug.

"You ain't boarding her with that twitchy kitchen girl?"

"No, no, don't be so simple." Hinton rolled his window back up, pulled a cigarillo out of his suit pocket, and struck a match across the dashboard. "This poor waif's mammy has obliged me to be her warden." He turned around to the back seat and blew a ring of smoke.

The confined space of the back seat was a coffin; not the plain pine boxes she'd witnessed at tenant funerals, but a plush black leather casket. She noticed the narrow wound on the bridge of Hinton's nose, the gash her father had planted. Whip was focused on the road ahead, his burly hands knotted around the steering wheel. In the rearview mirror, Molly could see his weary eyes were tainted like bruised green apples.

Hinton jabbered to himself as they drove on for a few miles, passing long strips of woods, idle farmlands, and lopsided cabins with smoke spilling from their cockeyed chimneys. On the left, they came upon rows of pecan trees, and a dirt road jutted out at the end of the orchard. A weathered bronze statue of a hunting dog clutching a bird in its mouth marked the entrance, and Whip turned in. The pecan grove created a tunnel over the passageway, and as they came out on the other side, sitting on a knob overlooking a line of cars was an alabaster manor house with wooden columns running along the front porch; three of the four were fancily carved flutes, but the fourth one, the pillar at the end nearest the parking lot, was a twisted cypress log. The slate sky was darkening as they neared the parked automobiles, each as colorful as a rooster's feathers.

"Go around to the kitchen. Take her up the backstairs to that far room where that buck-toothed gal used to stay. Make sure it ain't being utilized for business."

Before Molly could protest, Whip snatched her from the back seat, hauled her up the stairs, and inside the two-story house. He tapped on the bedroom door; after no reply, he opened the door and eased her onto the bed.

"You best rest while you can," Whip said. He opened the nightstand drawer, placed the soggy pouch inside it, and closed. "But don't you get no notions." He left the room, shutting the door behind him.

Molly heard the lock turn, and she lay still for a moment, finally free from the suffocating sedan. The mattress on the unmade brass bed nestled her snugly, but she crept out of it anyway. The room was practically larger than her family's whole cabin. She ran her hand along the satin wallcoverings, which were a gentle robin's egg blue. A ceramic washbasin sat on a marble vanity in between the chamber pot cabinet and the chest of drawers. There was a mirror in a gilded frame hanging above the limestone fireplace mantle, and a lone light bulb dropped on a frayed black cord from the tin panel ceiling.

In the center of the embossed wreath design was a rough-cut hole, as if a serpent had poked its head through the metal tile. Pulling back the white lace curtains, she saw a coupe parked next to the old hitching post; the gold two-door car had a large trunk but was shorter than Hinton's automobile.

Molly opened the nightstand drawer where Whip had hidden her mother's pouch. She doubted it carried anything useful like a dagger. Hinton had mentioned another girl who had lived in the frilly bedroom before her, and she wondered if the poor girl had kept her special perfumed toilet water, or her secret diary, in the drawer. As she reached for the nightstand drawer, she heard a commotion in the hallway and jumped back into bed, faking sleep. The bedroom door swung open. There was a click, and the room was filled with amber light. Molly shielded her eyes.

"What do you think?" Hinton declared walking into the bedroom with a woman while Whip stood in the doorway. Taking out another cigarillo, he dragged a match across the fireplace mantle and lit his smoke.

"I wouldn't exactly declare you *Père Noël* arriving early," the woman said, nearing the bed-side. Her accent was clipped but lustrous.

"I thought it was an ingenious idea," Hinton said. He blew his smoke rings toward the ceiling.

"Puffing a dainty cigar don't make you a gentleman or a genius." Sitting down on the edge of the bed, the woman complained about a rowdy group of men downstairs and the stopped-up plumbing. She put her hand on Molly's shoulder, nudging her onto her stomach. "Roll over, *chérie*."

Molly bit down on her lip and rolled over, hoping they'd pay her no mind. The woman reeked of gardenias, and she was wearing a long, layered silk dress like the town ladies wore to church, except Molly had never seen them wear anything cherry red, and their bosoms never bulged out of their corsets.

Peeling back Molly's nightgown, she exposed the lashes.

"Whip or her cunt mother?"

The overseer remained silent.

Spotting the oil lamp on the nightstand, Molly pictured smashing Hinton over the head and escaping out the window. She'd drive off in the gold car like it was a chariot, never mind that she didn't know how to operate an automobile or that Whip would be on her in a flash.

"I best ramble on," Hinton said, grounding out his cigarillo on his heel and tossing it into the fireplace.

"Roll on back, darling."

The woman's powdered, broad face reminded Molly of a porcelain cat.

"A healthy dose will settle her in," she said, stroking Molly's cheek. "I need my kit." The woman stood up and stomped her left foot on the floor three times. "Sally!"

"Hellfire, that dimwitted housemaid can't hear you from all the way up here." Hinton laughed.

"What you don't know." The woman rearranged the combs in her reddish blond hair, straightening her upswept headdress.

"I know some rich gadabout will pay top dollar for a poke of her gash," Hinton said.

"She's got a saucy *derrière*, no doubt. But can she sing?" the woman said. "You know any tunes besides gospel, gal?"

"W-what?" Molly mumbled.

"Can you sing anything besides 'Amazing Grace?' Jesus quenches the ambiance in the parlor."

"N-no, ma'am,"

"That's alright, we'll teach you to moan the copulating blues." The woman faced Hinton. "So?"

"Put her to work and pay me my five hundred out of her cut," Hinton said, inspecting his thinning hair in the mirror. "She's a tenant girl. She's gotta pay her board."

"Oh, we don't tolerate moochers at my house." The woman pulled a jeweled snuff tin out of her bodice and took two quick snorts. She grumbled again about the penny-pinching lumber wahoos downstairs but bragged about a Wall Street gang visiting soon.

Hearing their sketchy plans, Molly couldn't decide if it meant that in no time she'd be free or that only her salvation was Alma Mae's return. She wondered how the Lord could have cast her over to two wicked sinners, but she believed beseeching him now would only make her weak, her blubbering prayer working as a silly cry for pity.

A thundering came down the hallway, and a young red-headed girl dashed into the room, setting a bag down in front of the woman.

"That's good, Sal," the woman said. "Now rustle up my shea butter."

The young girl turned and darted out of the room again like a bolt of red lighting.

Hinton put on his black bowler. "I don't believe Ms. Lynn would be too delighted in holding my Sunday dinner much longer."

"She most likely wouldn't be delighted in holding anything of yours for very long," the woman said, with a wink at Molly as Whip and Hinton left the room.

Rummaging through the violet paisley satchel the girl had brought, the woman pulled out a vial and a rectangular silver metal box. She opened the box and took out a syringe. The tube and needle were the same kind Doc K had used when he'd given Molly a shot after a rusty harrow sliced open her foot. Alma Mae had made her father ride her to the clinic when Molly had been unable to help tend to their tobacco plants and her mother had spent her Saturday afternoon picking off horn-worms and crushing the large green caterpillars underfoot.

"Excuse my manners, darling. I'm Pauline Mercier, Madam Mercier," the woman said, extending her hand.

"Molly . . . Molly Lingo."

"*Enchantée*," Madam Mercier said, shaking her hand. She

released her grip and picked the syringe up off the table. "You read, darling?"

"Yes, ma'am."

"I'll find you some magazines," the woman said, loading the hollow barrel with the fluid from the emerald ampule. "Kitchen starts at 6:00 AM, or so they tell me. Sal will fetch you." She lifted up the bottom of Molly's nightgown and jabbed the syringe into her buttock.

Molly felt the prick of the needle, and as Madam Mercier cast an incantation, a blessedness passed through her, unbinding her every muscle. A gentle fatigue draped over her, and her eyelids bounced up and down as if driven by invisible wires.

"This'll pamper you like the kindly sister you wish you had." Madam Mercier's face became a creamy blur.

A light peace streamed over her skin. Appearing in a thready streak of sweet pale smoke, the brown-haired woman stood next to the bed, shrouded in midnight blue. She placed her palms on Molly's belly. A soothing hum filled the notch above her breastbone, and she could taste honey on the tip of her tongue. Molly was sure the healing power of the Holy Ghost surged through the young woman's chapped hands. Her eyes fluttered back in her head, and the cozy mattress swallowed her whole, shielding her from the commotion downstairs.

Chapter 6

By Sunday evening, Cotton was sure he had the crabs. There was a peculiar tingling in his crotch, and all he wanted to do was to take a back scratcher to the sweaty crevice between his nut sack and thighs. Scrubbing his balls with a good lice shampoo would kill the parasites, though if pus started dripping from his dick, he'd have to visit the Jew doctor. But that was a problem for another day. Tonight, he had to salvage an unsuccessful weekend of selling. Hawking stripes to county prisons was covering his draw but not much else. He tugged at the zipper on his trousers and scanned the crowd in the parlor room—it resembled a freshman mixer more than a brothel.

The nitpicking yard managers and procurement agents he'd been hosting for three days were clumped up around the fireplace, sipping cups of spicy ginger punch they didn't know Cotton had spiked with Huck's shine. On the other side of the room, the whores—blotto since Friday night—lounged on the davenports gossiping and flashing their tits at each other. He grabbed the pitcher and walked into the middle of the fireplace conversation.

"Here you go, fellas, let me top these off," Cotton said, filling their tin cups before they had a chance to object. They were all still wearing their heavy twill field britches and flannel shirts, refusing his suggestion to change into outfits more suited for indoor recreation. "Where's Carson and Roberts?"

"That milquetoast pair retired as soon as they got a belly full of fried chicken," Odom replied with a slur of tipsy bravado. "Probably having wet dreams about another platter of breast meat."

The other three men—Lewis, Jones, and McEwan—laughed like they hadn't all been asleep the last two nights before the moon had risen above the treetops. But Odom was the head of purchasing for Pine Hill Timber Company and those three guffawed at every wisecrack he'd made.

"Or they might be hankerin' for thighs and legs, the way they was swoonin' over that nigga cook. We may need to check they aren't pokin' her in the smokehouse."

The trio burst out in shrieks. Noticing that Odom took another sip of punch to conceal his grin, Cotton joined in their laughter and slapped the head purchasing agent on the back. The lanky curmudgeon was taking bids for next year's order of picks and shovels and every tractor supply company in four states was conniving to win the business. At least he'd stop carping about the hunting guides who "rattled those antlers like a mousy widow," the stew which was "not fit for a dog's breakfast," the pillows that "reeked of sour milk," and the front porch. When Cotton had arrived, all six of his guests were bunched around the cypress log that served as the temporary fourth column. He'd listened for ten minutes to Odom berating the asininity of the solution, "like a mule's ass sewed together with a grapevine," and he'd spent another ten minutes convincing him to come inside because the lodge was the only place to sleep and eat in Perry County. Thankfully, after two or three punches, they'd started talking about pussy, and colored pussy at that.

"You gentlemen seem like you're in the frame of mind for a last night of mirth-making. How about some cards?" Cotton asked, addressing the circle of men but looking only at Odom. He'd been trying to get them to them to the poker table and skin them for a few bucks, not clean them out, but enough to cover the cost of his liquor. The only other marks he'd seen were a bumpkin with a bowler and a brute following behind him like a calf trailing his mom, but the pair had left soon after they'd arrived.

Odom tasted his spiked ginger punch and glanced around with a miffed frown for the English pointers that had farted and stunk up the parlor. Backing away from Cotton, the other three mimicked the prickly head purchasing agent.

"I can play pinochle at home," Odom said with the same mockery he used to characterize the designer of the cypress log column.

"That wasn't what I was intending." Cotton advanced on the ring and raised the pitcher to fill McEwan's cup, but the stubby Scottish yard manager covered it with his hand.

"What's wrong? You ready for beddy-bye?" Odom thrust his empty tin cup forward, and Lewis and Jones followed along.

"Nah, I'll get loudly," McEwan said sticking his cup over the top of the others.

One of the girls, Frida, fell off the davenport and the other parlor girls giggled and snorted.

"See, you're getting those shy young girls all amorous feeling." Cotton emptied the last of the pitcher into their cups, making sure Odom's was full to the brim.

"Bet you could use a slice of wet, warm amorous pie, Mac," Odom said, not hiding his wiseacre grin.

The first day out in the field McEwan had stayed out of the conversation and walked a few paces behind the rest of group. Every evening, he went out after dinner, and Cotton had heard him playing the harmonica as the Scotsman strolled around the pecan grove. Lewis and Jones told him that McEwan had lost his wife in a house fire right after he started with the company.

"Frida told me she was hoping you could give her a few tips on playing the mouth harp," Cotton said.

"Nah, I don't know."

"Sure you do, you could do a duet," Cotton elbowed the Scotsman. "And it would save her from getting in any more trouble."

"What do you say?"

"She gets hit with demerits for not mingling with the guests."

"Like school?" Lewis asked, tilting his head to the side.

"Yes sir, like finishing school."

"What sort of mingling?" Jones pushed his glasses up on his nose and studied the drunk whores.

"Socializing. Shooting the breeze. That's it."

"Hell, we can do that." Lewis poked McEwan in the kidney, making the Scotsman squirm.

Odom blinked a few times and turned away to look at the dwindling fire.

"Come on over here, ladies." Cotton motioned to the lounging girls, then pivoted back to his guests. "Besides, tonight's entertainment is on me."

After straightening their hairdos and the necklines of their dresses so their breasts were perky, the crew of girls teetered over to the men at the fireplace. Odom smiled and shook his head as two girls nuzzled up to him. Cotton hadn't discussed running a tab for the sporting, the madam had been busy, but the lodging, the meals, and hunting were all being billed directly to Tri-State. He'd paid out of pocket for Huck's shine and his first two nights of screwing. He'd fucked Frida and Emma on Friday night after their accordion and yodeling performance sounded as pitiful as a country church choir. On Saturday night, Evelyn—the dumpy one with a notched knife scar on her tit—wheedled her way into a suck and a poke, and not long after he'd come back downstairs, Marie—the olive-skinned girl with a hint of Creole in her—cornered him in the parlor, and he bent her over the chaise lounge.

Within the time needed for Cotton to get the fire blazing— select the driest logs, place them crossways across the top, and stoke it with the pewter iron—Frida had coaxed McEwan upstairs, Emma had pulled Lewis from the parlor, and Evelyn had latched onto Jones, herding him up to her room. Cotton was left with Odom, Marie, and the two whores he hadn't fucked yet—Viola and Pearl—who had the purchasing agent sandwiched between them.

"All roads are open," Cotton said, retrieving Huck's shine from his suit coat pocket. He spun off the metal screw lid and handed the green glass jar to Odom.

Pressing the wide mouth container to his lips, the purchasing agent leaned his head back and chugged two or three large gulps. "Woo-wee," Odom coughed. He shoved the jar back at Cotton, doubled over, and hacked for air. When he straightened himself back up, his eyes were red and watery. He spat a wad of phlegm into the fire. "Good God damn," he said, seizing Viola and Pearl around their waists and steering them upstairs.

Cotton took a swig and offered a drink to Marie. The black-haired girl guzzled down all but the last drops of the corn liquor, and before she set down the jar, he gripped her butt with both hands. With a push from his pelvis, he drove her towards the chaise lounge from last night.

"Upstairs," she said, nudging him away with the empty jar and wiggling free.

"C'mon." Cotton pictured her slender waist and her round ass cheeks in the firelight.

"No, sir, Madam Mercier don't hold with peter tracks on her imported Henrietta fabric." Marie tugged at his shirt sleeve.

"Alright," he said, allowing her to tow him to her bedroom. He'd watch the busty madam who ran the place saunter in and out of the parlor all weekend, barking at the unruly whores. In her beaded evening dresses, she could've passed for a background extra in a Hollywood picture show, most likely sleeping with the producer. There wasn't any gain in irritating the boss lady, who could charge a weekend of whoring to his company the same as extra platters of fried chicken.

There was a tin of prophylactics on the nightstand.

"Hold still, sweetheart," Cotton said, patting Marie's ass. The Creole girl's backside was arched upwards and her feet spread apart as she propped herself up in front of the fireplace, gripping the edge of the wobbly end table for support. He scurried across the room naked, snatched the silver tin of 3 Merry Widows, and hurried back to his position. There'd been only one log in the basket. The firelight might fade before he slipped on his condom. Sliding the thin sheath over the tip of his erection, he checked Marie's image in the bureau mirror. It was how he imagined he would've fucked his cousin's fiancé in the powder room at Creekside. That was uncomplicated, but it was difficult for him to conceive of M.K. arranged in a similar stance.

There were three or four loud bangs on the bedroom door. "Marie."

The girl squealed and stood upright.

"Marie," a woman demanded from the hallway.

Cotton recognized the narrow punch of the madam's voice, and his penis softened in his hand.

"*Pouffiasse*, have you got that swollen-headed salesman in here?" the madam asked, thumping the bedroom door harder.

"*Oui*, Madam," Marie replied, covering her breasts and pubis with her hands.

"Shit fire," Cotton said, tossing the loose condom up in the air. He jerked the bedroom door open. "Did you mean Captain Arnold?"

The madam stood in the doorway like a barbed wire barricade; her arms folded across her chest. "*Pardonnez-moi*, but come get your man out of my parlor, Captain," the madam replied,

"Which one?"

"That skinflint bastard who's driving Pearl around likes

she's a wheelbarrow." The madam's scowl cropped up from beneath her face powder.

Putting on his trousers without concern for his pecker getting stuck in the zipper, Cotton accompanied her downstairs, buttoning his shirt and listening to the madam squawk about Viola heaving fried chicken and corn liquor all over the rugs. She threatened to fetch a bouncer if he didn't stop the sorry drunken fucker from tearing up the household.

"No need," Cotton said, confused about who the madam used for security, but certain she had ample protection.

The pair arrived at the entrance to the parlor, and the madam pointed to Odom balling Pearl like he was hammering a fence post into the hard ground. Cotton stepped past the glaring procuress.

In the center of the room, the head of purchasing for Pine Valley Timber stood behind Pearl, holding her by the ankles and raising her pelvis up at an angle while she balanced herself on her head. With each of Odom's thrust, she teetered from side-to-side. Cotton recalled screwing a Punjabi girl in Paris this way, but it was more trouble than it was worth, and the nimble young gal had keeled over before he could finish.

"Good God damn," Odom said, turning toward Cotton and releasing his grasp of Pearl. The willowy whore collapsed into a contorted knot. He picked up a jug off the floor, knocked back a swig, and handed it to Cotton.

Sniffing the spout, Cotton didn't think the oily pine tar hooch would pass the blue flame test. He took a nip—closer to turpentine than booze. A night of drinking this rotgut potion would turn a parish priest into a howling lunatic. "That'll make your pecker pop out," he said, concealing the stoneware jug behind his back.

"You're damn straight." Odom seesawed from side-to-side. "Two dollars a shovel, a thousand spades, a thousand squares, and a thousand trenchers."

"OK," Cotton said, figuring the size of the commission check on an order that large. The most he'd sold was a hundred to his uncle and those had been at list price, a dollar-and-a-half per shovel.

"That carries a Mercury dime in each one for my pension," he said, his hard-on protruding from under his belly.

"We're all jake with that." Cotton figured at a third higher than list price he could afford a ten-cent kickback.

"Oh, yessir, I see all you peddlers, slip, slip, slippin' 'round. I know Uncle's army ain't buying like he was when we were killing Krauts."

"We appreciate your business. We surely do," Cotton said, as if he was conversing with a lost toddler in the park. He studied Odom's naked gangly frame and decided he preferred convincing the purchasing agent to walk up to bed rather than wait for him to pass out.

Lurching away from Cotton, Odom swayed backward and plopped down on the madam's davenport. "You angling on bagging that state deal for all those crawlers and road patrols?"

"I'm courting 'em hard," Cotton replied in a strong roll call voice, intending to cover up his bewilderment about what state deal he was referring to. Tri-State didn't hold the jobber contract for any manufacturer of tractors and the only road patrols they represented were Hogan's mule graders.

"I bet you scheming some sorta audacious angle. I hear the salesman lands this bid will be living the life of Riley." The drunken crank was leaking sweat and jism onto the imported fabric. "Yessir, that's what I hear."

"I'm not putting sums in my bankbook yet." Cotton stepped closer to the sofa. "What else you hear?" Tractor-selling functioned the same as the stock market. Only nitwits speculated on which shares to invest their capital in—the big dough was earned from insider tips. Living happy-go-lucky would be swell, but it'd also be nice to stop living out of a trunk, shacking up in boarding houses or dodging his folks like his happiness was still dependent on his father's moods.

"Plenty, plenty, plenty, my brother's college—" Without warning, Odom's head bobbled about, his jaw dropped, and his eyes opened wide, staring out past Cotton, searching for something on the horizon. He snorted and keeled over onto his side.

The madam entered the parlor from behind Cotton. "Get him up to his room, Mr. Isaac, then fetch up Pearl." Madam Mercier said, instructing the colored man who eased in next. "Make sure you set him down on the bed easy, but don't worry about tucking him in, or anything."

With a deep, content breath, the stocky hunting guide lifted Odom to his feet, raised his limp body over his right shoulder, steadied his load, and carried the snoring purchasing agent out of the parlor.

"You better hope vinegar and seltzer removes these stains," the madam said, inspecting her fine davenport.

"I'm certain cleaning peter tracks ain't an unencountered problem."

"Would you prefer Tri-State Supply Company pay the cum cleaning charges?" the madam asked.

"If we had to, that'd be jake," Cotton replied. "Along with the rest of the tonight's frivolity."

"Jake yourself."

"Of course, I'd pay a cash gratuity to the girls." It was late, but Cotton could still visualize his bankroll hidden in the drawer lining of his wardrobe trunk. "And you."

"You make it square with me," the madam said, holding up her lamp to examine Cotton's face. "I'll handle my girls and your invoice."

"Your joint, your rules." Cotton smiled, feeling the glass lamp glow on his cheeks and the madam's stare, her waning mask of flaking makeup and her sneer. There was little choice other than to pay her more than a modest tip. The lodge produced at a better rate than the slickest sales catalog. He'd circle back around to follow-up with Odom for the straight skinny on the state deal after the guilt had vanished and only the braggadocious rush of memory remained. Give him a tip on handling whorehouse bed bugs. Tracking down Archibald was his top priority. His old army buddy had all sorts of connections in manufacturing. Modern earthmoving equipment was making men and mules obsolete. He'd see if they could meet in Atlanta on Arch's next trip through town. Private rail cars could make their own schedule. If he could land a jobber contract for a line of crawler tractors and road graders, the bosses in Birmingham might be impressed enough with Cotton's initiative to promote him to sales manager.

Chapter 7

Within two or three weeks, the practice of learning a new routine worked like a salve on her wounds. Each morning, well before sunrise, Sally woke her up, and while Molly dressed, clearing her mind from the mist of the madam's potions, the plump redhead chattered on about life in the Lodge, loud enough to annoy the slumbering girls down the hall but not to wake the madam. She told Molly about the Watts', the family who cooked the meals and guided the hunters, "they're as smooth and hard as river rocks," about the six girls that worked in the parlor, "conniving cunny mostly," and the lodge guests, "we got us a new load of dapper Dans coming in from Memphis this evening."

The day began in earnest in the cookhouse, and Sally and Molly worked alongside Lizzy Watts and her two daughters, preparing the identical breakfast every morning: biscuits, grits, and country ham with red-eye gravy. Lizzy ruled the cookhouse like a queen, and Hinton and Madam Mercier deferred to her reign. The unyielding mother produced a feast of food, running the cook-house like a cotton mill shuttle loom, knowing how to control it with the balance of love and stern indifference.

"Sal, you keepin' those grits stirred?" Lizzy Watts said, more telling than asking.

"Ouch," Sally said, sticking her fingers into the pot and licking them clean. "Need a dash of something. Where's the whatchamacallit?"

Molly shredded last night's leftover fried chicken into morsels, stripping the bones clean with a paring knife. The larder was jammed with dry goods and meats, deliveries from the general store and the butcher arriving two or three times a week, but Lizzy didn't waste a scrap. Any leftovers were fed to the guests, the staff, the hunting dogs or the hogs. Skillet wouldn't know how to cope with such abundance, but Alma Mae would've beaten Sally with a leather strap on a daily basis.

"Keep your rotten paws to yourself, and you know where the salt be. Your sweet whore momma must've bounced you off a Storyville cobblestone."

The Watts girls, copper droplets of their mother, giggled as they kneaded the dough for another tray of cathead biscuits. Their mother tapped the butt of her fork on top of the cast-iron stove and shook her head twice. The young Watts girls snickering stopped, and they began kneading faster.

Sally pulled the salt canister down from the rack above the stove. "We having stew for lunch?"

"Chicken and okra gumbo." Lizzy Watts tended the slabs of sizzling country ham.

"Mm, how about dinner?"

"What night is it?"

"Tuesday, oh, wait, is it Wednesday? Yep, it's Wednesday."

"So?"

Sally doctored the bubbling pot of stone mill grits with salt. "I ain't seen Mr. Isaiah. He and your boys must be down at the smokehouse."

"One last guess. Ribs or pulled pork?"

"We had ribs for those insurance fellas, so I guess pulled pork."

"Except Madam Mercier says the boss man of this Memphis crowd decides last minute he's in the mood for ribs. Forget the trouble tradin' with that grocer's low-down boy." Lizzy lifted the searing hot country ham out of the skillet, the sizzling grease popping on the back of her hand. The fatty chunk slipped onto the tarnished plank floor, but she snatched it up, flinging it onto the serving tray. "At least you was only bounced once," she said, pointing the slick tines of her bone-handled fork at Sally.

Lizzy only cooked five different dinners: fried chicken, chicken and dumplings, fried pork chops, and either smoked pork butts or baby back ribs. The guests rotated so they never had the same meal twice, and the pattern enabled her to improvise with seasonal side dishes like collard greens with ham hocks or fried apples and cabbage. The whole lodge ran on a similar pulse, producing a rhythmic semblance.

After breakfast, Isaiah Watts and his three boys led the hunters off in mule-drawn wagons, and the girls straightened the guest rooms, making sure not to wake Madam Mercier. Lunch was served in bowls: ham and navy beans, apple and pork stew, or chicken gumbo. Once the guests left for their afternoon hunt, Sally served the madam and the parlor girls breakfast in bed, while Molly and the Watts girls, Hettie and Mary, started working on supper. At mid-afternoon, before the upstairs housekeeping, Molly had her only respite from chores.

Reading the daily mail was essential to Madam Mercier's routine, and the mailbox was a long walk from the manor house. Sally dallied too much, and Hettie and Mary couldn't be trusted with the madam's correspondence, so they assigned the errand to Molly. Besides her nightly doses, it was the only grace she felt all day. Venturing out of the front door, Molly strode down the road. The brisk wind saturated her cheeks, and the splintery crush of the leaves revived her spirit, proving she was alive. Hettie or Mary always trailed her in the background, walking a few rows deep in the grove. At first, she saw them as spies, but later, she waved at them as they frolicked beside her. She absorbed each rise and turn in the tight orchard road, each with a promise of Alma Mae and Stanley riding up in a fancy sedan with a stranger, her undiscovered grandfather from Moab Mountain, coming to rescue her. But heeding Whip's warning, she returned to the porch, crippled by the stark winter grove, cursing Sally's blabbering.

In the evening, Sally rang a gong that she claimed came from Java, or Borneo, and Madam Mercier and the tittering parlor girls strolled in their slinky evening gowns past the lodge guests to their private dining room, filling the air with brassy perfume and salacious winks. After supper, Sally and Molly cleared the plates, and Lizzy made certain Hettie and Mary remained in the kitchen; even the most genteel lodge guests considered the radiant kitchen girls with deeper interest after a few shots of rye. Once the serious drinking commenced, the Watts brothers escorted their sisters back to their cabin next to pens and the smokehouse.

When the grandfather clock in the vestibule chimed eight, the men gathered in the parlor for the entertainment, puffing on Ybor City cigars and imbibing Hinton's home-brew, but Molly retreated to her upstairs bedroom to meet the madam for their nighttime ritual. Once she slipped into her nightgown, she would pour them each glasses of Oloroso, the madam's favorite sherry, and sit on the side of her bed, sipping the sweet wine as the madam laid out all the ingredients from her silver box on the marble vanity.

A howl of laughter filtered up from the parlor.

"Damn, if there's nothing not funnier than a drunk hee-hawing at his own stale joke and a doped-up whore encouraging him," the madam said, screwing the needle onto the chamber.

"Yes, ma'am," Molly said. "This bunch is awful loud."

"That Memphis fellow is a ripe pain in my petunia." She slid the plunger into the chamber, tested it, and sat it back down on the vanity. "Was Lizzy upset about scrounging ribs?"

"Oh, no, ma'am." Eying the sleek syringe, Molly felt the exhaustion from the day's chores devour her.

"If she was, you'd tell me?"

"Of course, yes, ma'am."

The madam savored her Oloroso and went on grumbling about the Memphis guests.

A dull headache started behind Molly's eyes, and she stared at the ampule, gleaming like an electric star in a milky marble sky. She drank the last of her sherry.

"Wait until I tell Lizzy about the Wall Street crowd next week. No fried yard bird or swine for those gentlemen, they got to have Porterhouses." Madam Mercier topped off her crystal goblet. "You'd tell Lizzy for me, wouldn't you?"

"Yes, ma'am, if you'd like me to," Molly said, wondering how many sips the madam would take before she picked up the ampule and filled the syringe. Molly had memorized the process, and was confident she could complete most of it. She was nervous about filling the syringe and expelling the air bubbles, yet she could if she had to, but she doubted she'd ever had the moxie for the finishing step—injecting herself.

"If you aren't the most good-natured gal. You know, your first time won't be any different than a bad bout of the green-apple-quick-steps—the discomfort passes like a midnight trip to the privy in wintertime," the madam said, picking up the syringe and filling it. "I've conjured up a heartening story to tell before your auction."

"Story?"

"Something to drive up the bidding, a damsel-in-distress tear-jerker."

"After the thing—the auction—will I be able to go home?"

The madam squirted a small amount of fluid from the syringe as her last test. "Go home?"

Hearing her question repeated back, interrupting the procedure, heightened the throbbing across her brow. Another loud peal of laughter came from the parlor.

"I thought you were expecting your mother to come for you." Madam Mercier said, rising from the chair and turning off the overhead light, leaving only the glow of the bedside lamp.

Molly hung her right leg off the side of the bed.

Madam Mercier cradled Molly's leg, easing a delicate finger

in the gap next to her big toe. "Sal has been waiting for four or five years for her mother. I'm not sure Alma Mae is any more reliable than Cassie."

Feeling the burn in the tissue between her toes, Molly realized that another day had passed at the lodge.

Chapter 8

The morning the Wall Street guests were due to arrive, the weekend before Christmas, the grocer's son delivered the news to Lizzy.

"My old man gave me a lot of do's and don'ts about these crates, but he never said nothing about arguing with no sassy darkie," the delivery boy said.

"You ain't long enough out of knickers to be talking like that." Lizzy said, jabbing at a hunk of country ham and glaring at the delivery boy as Molly and the other girls went about their morning duties.

"Listen here, when I'm told to carry these here crates from our cooler to your kitchen, I just do what I'm told. Maybe you need to remember your place and do the same." The lanky teen tucked a thumb under one of his suspenders and stepped further into the kitchen and away from the dim service doorway, the only entrance the Watts Family had ever used.

"And I'm telling you, those crates don't belong here. Sally, go wake up Ms. Pauline," Lizzy said, with the calm of reminding the girls to set the cane syrup on the table.

The plump redhead dropped her spoon on the floor. Molly looked up from her mound of shredded chicken. Now leaning against the Watts girls' working table, the town boy looked identical to every other merchant's son that lived in Scots Station, not tan and worn like a farmer's child but the bloodless pale of the parlor girls' faces dabbed in ivory powder.

The delivery boy reclined back, advancing closer to the Watts girls. Hettie flashed a half-grin. Mary nudged her hip. They pressed down firmer on the moist lumps of flour.

"Go on now, Sally, don't be a square biscuit." Lizzy stepped away from the smoking iron skillet, refusing to look away from the slanted stare of the delivery boy.

"What?" Sally shuffled toward the door to the main house, and then back toward the stove, picking her stirring spoon off the floor and wiping it across the front of her dress. She held the wooden utensil close to her chest.

The delivery boy dipped two fingers into a stray pile of flour and flicked a milky spray at the twins.

Lizzy's grip went taut around her kitchen fork, the thick butt-end jutting out from her fist.

Molly recognized the boy's ratty hair, and remembered seeing him around his father's store. Preparing to volunteer to wake up Madam Mercier, Molly considered the consequences of rousing the slumbering madam. She grabbed up her knife.

The tarnished gold bone-handle trembled in Lizzy's hand.

"I'm sorry, Ms. Lizzy," Molly said, wiping her hands on her apron and stashing her paring knife. She approached the pair. "Madam Mercier told me to tell you that this Wall Street bunch coming in tonight only ate something called Porterhouses. Whatever that is?"

Molly gave a slight schoolgirl smile to the delivery boy, and he replied with a squinty smirk.

"They're prime-cut beefsteaks," he said, thrusting his pointy chin at Ms. Lizzy.

"Beefsteaks?" Lizzy glanced at the stack of crates.

"Yep, I got a crate of Porterhouses, one of those Delmonico's, a couple of tenderloin roast, and some flatirons for breakfast."

"What in God's creation?" Lizzy shook her head and turned her back to the grinning grocer's son. "You girls stack them crates in the corner."

"Top of the morning to you," the delivery boy said, tipping his cap to the twins and strutting out of the kitchen.

"I'm sorry again," Molly said, stacking the crates of beef in the corner before Sally and the Watts girls could move. "I'll talk to Madam Mercier when I bring her the mail."

"I ain't got no mind to what I'll be cooking or how I'm cooking it," Lizzy said, working to salvage the charred slices of country ham. "But I ain't giving the devil a foothold this morning."

Most afternoons when Molly brought the mail to Madam Mercier, she'd find her still in her nightclothes propped up in her canopy bed or reclining on her chaise lounge in front of the bay window, but today, the madam was dressed and sitting at her secretary desk, studying her ledger.

"Oh, good, the post," Madam Mercier said, looking up as Molly entered the madam's suite, which was above the sun porch at the opposite end of the hall from hers.

"Yes, ma'am," Molly said, handing the bundle to the madam.

"With any luck, it's more reservation deposits than bills. Maybe some Christmas cards if we've been naughty enough." Madam Mercier stood up. "Everything go OK at breakfast? Those tight-wad insurance cranks get gone?"

"Without a hitch," Molly said, omitting their grumbling about the lumpy bland grits, the burnt country ham, and not being able to talk business with Hinton, who had a habit of not appearing for those who wanted to see him and for hovering over those who didn't.

"Good riddance, stingy louts prefer a cold shower over hot pussy," the madam said, scolding a misbehaving child.

Hearing her firm hard tone reminded Molly of Alma Mae's voice when she disciplined her and Stanley or rebuked her father for any number of misdeeds, except the madam didn't keep a leather strap hidden behind her back.

"At least it gave the girls a rest before the Edelman Brothers' hotshot army invades. Did Parker's make the delivery?" the madam asked, sorting through the envelopes.

"Yes, ma'am, before sun up." Molly noticed the madam's

new stylish lavender dress, the hemline stopping at her knee and exposing her calf.

"Lizzy not too upset?"

"No, ma'am, but she was wondering if there are any particular directions—beefsteak cooking recipes—you want her to follow?"

The madam sat the mail down on her desk and rummaged through her bookshelf. She pulled down a red book and handed it to Molly.

"Easy enough to pan fry them in a cast iron skillet, but I'm sure there's something in the *Fannie Farmer* that help gussie them up with a tad of *je ne sais quoi*." Madam Mercier walked over to her bed and sorted through a pile of dresses she had laid out. "Otto and Jacob's gang are swift with a buck. Rich Yankees make a gal spread her legs lickety-split." The madam picked up a dress from the heap and held it in front of her. "What do you think of these?"

Molly knotted her lips sealed. The dandelion yellow shift resembled a chiffon croaker sack.

"Don't you adore it?" The madam said, tossing it down and picking up another one to model. "I ordered these at Marshall Field's in Chi-town when I met Tyrus for our summer *rendezvous*. Which do you like better?"

Raising the thick dog-eared cookbook to shield her face, Molly studied the shapeless steel blue dress covered in tassels and sequins. She'd never picked out dresses before, and none of these looked like anything she'd ever seen in Scots Station or that the parlor girls had worn before.

"It's hard to choose, isn't it?" The madam threw the blue one back and pulled out a baggy black one.

Molly had thought it was a velvet horse blanket. She watched as Madam Mercier postured in front of the mirror. This madam's suite had similar dark cherry wood furnishings and blue wall-paper as her room. But this afternoon it seemed far-off, like Molly was a wooden figurine in a dollhouse, and the mischievous little girl toying with her couldn't decide what part she was supposed to play. Eager to return to the kitchen and give Ms. Lizzy the recipes she needed, she low-ered the book. "Yes, ma'am, besides, I don't know nothing much about choosing dresses."

"Don't worry, darling, for the auction, I've got an outfit more befitting a Southern belle. Bring the *Fannie Farmer* to Lizzy and pray the Edelmans' visit turns out more pleasing than Grant's siege at Vicksburg."

To learn more about how the emerging Jazz Age shaped Molly's story, subscribe to Southern Fried Karma's YouTube channel, Fugitive Views.

Chapter 9

In the lobby of the Georgian Terrace hotel, amidst the red chenille sofas and hand-painted Oriental vases, Cotton's mind simmered with tales of the people sharing his space while he waited for Archibald Carrel, his former lieutenant.

The Senator's wife was skimming the newspaper and ogling the colored bellman.

The pudding-faced bank vice president squeezed his felt trilby while waiting in front of the elevator for chairman of the board.

The bearded Italian architect drank a glass of freshly squeezed orange juice and admired the same junior bellman as the Senator's banjo-eyed wife.

Sipping his second cup of coffee, cooled by a splash from the half-pint he had discovered in his suit coat, Cotton checked on the lobby messenger boy to ensure he was still on the lookout for Archibald. During their Dublin campaign, back in '22 or '23, Arch and he had used the lobby of The Shelbourne as a sanctuary from the round-up of Mick buskers and grifters on Grafton Street. Before that, the open patio lobby of the Pera Palace Hotel in Constantinople had served as their refuge from the daggers and the strays infesting the European district. Starting at Camp Gordon in '17, they'd served together in the Great War, the Greek-Turkish War, the Irish Civil War and the Banana War in Honduras, sharing endless missions until each one became a heap of clandestine memory. Meeting with Archibald seemed the most logical first step. It was better than beginning with his father. He was optimistic his comrade could guide him down the right path to securing an earthmoving dealership. It had to be simpler than dealing with a Sicilian fruit grower from New Orleans.

Arch had always described his family business with the vague phrase "investment banking." Cotton knew the Carrels owned an amalgamation of insurance companies, trust companies, and industrial banks. Arch had said his family served as "the capital underwriting syndicate for those who preferred dealing with their own tribe."

The messenger boy waved at Cotton and ran towards him. "Bellman goin' upstairs to fetch down a giant steamer now, Captain," he said, reporting his findings and holding out his palm.

"And?" Cotton asked.

"And Odell says it's Lieutenant Carrel." He stuck his hand closer to Cotton's chin.

"You sure it ain't Al Jolson?" Digging into his pants pocket, Cotton pulled out his leather coin pouch.

"Nah, Mr. Odell doesn't beat his gums like that."

After Cotton dropped a few wheat pennies into the boy's hungry palm, the messenger scurried off. The Georgian Terrace was a trolley car ride down Peachtree Street from the state capital and everyone in the vicinity aimed to wet their beaks—it seemed to follow the tractor-selling business. A few days ago, he'd called on Odom, figuring a week or ten days was sufficient time to let him recover his appetite. After Cotton slipped him the brown manila envelope for his pension, the old crank talked so long about the state deal for the crawlers that Cotton had a hard time staying awake. Corley Brewer was the big gun that controlled the bids. According to Odom, Cotton needed the Alabama Road Superintendent "like a dead man needs a coffin." He'd left the waspy purchasing agent's office and sent a telegram to the Superintendent and another to his old army buddy, arranging a meeting the next time his private railcar stopped in Atlanta. Spotting Arch exiting the elevator, Cotton hurried past the pudding-faced banker to greet his chum. "Finally, man and mountain meet again."

"Cap, I'm sorry for being in such a rush," Arch said, setting down his grip. The bellman trailing behind him stopped.

"No apology needed." Cotton extended his hand. The compatriots shook hands and slapped each other on the shoulder. "How was your stay?"

"Lousy. All the well-heeled money is after the next snazzy soda pop." Arch turned to address the bellman. "Odell, I'll check out in short order and that trunk goes with me to Terminal station, posthaste." He peeled two dollars off a roll of bills and handed them to the bellman, who hoisted the flat-top steamer onto his back and marched out the front door. Stuffing the plump roll into his pocket, he shifted back to Cotton. "You're standing pretty tall."

"Yeah, yeah, tip-top. Same to you, Joe Brooks as always," Cotton replied. The two men were dressed in similar dark brown double-breasted suits. Arch's wool bowler and the scar below his dark sideburns were the only features setting them apart. "Have you considered my telegram?"

"Of course. We've got connections with the engine makers, Maxwell, Oliver. They're all building crawlers. If you'd like, I can make some introductions, drop you a list of contacts, straight-shooting hayseed inventor types."

"That'd be swell. I'm on the inside rail—riding a winner right out of the gate," Cotton crowed, unable to stop himself from imitating the assurance of a tonic peddler.

"Easy enough. I'll phone my office from the next station, have my gal put it in the post. Where they sending it? Home or office?"

"Either one, I guess." The hotel staff swirled about the lobby, and the other guests were immersed in their private dramas. Cotton had accepted the notion that at one point he'd have to bring his father in on his idea, but invariably it became a task for tomorrow. Lucius Arnold was a devout teetotaler when it came to partaking in risk, and he'd unearth the miscalculations in his son's business approach like he was protecting Laius from Oedipus.

"Are you planning on buying a demonstrator model?" Arch asked, glancing at the line to check-out.

"I intend something like that," Cotton replied, his voice mellowing. If he'd told Arch that his primary selling tool was a backwoods brothel, his army buddy's perspective of the deal may have soured. "What's a demonstrator run?"

"Five or six grand, but an advanced order like that'll be a real sweetener."

"Nothing works like action." Cotton couldn't calculate how many nights of whoring he could fund for six grand.

"You moving on from hawking shovels and prison stripes?"

"You pegged it, advancing to the head of the ranks." Stretching his hand up toward the ceiling, a buoyant beat returned to Cotton's voice. He'd make a visit out to Creekside and talk with his mother about his earthmoving equipment idea. She'd see the wisdom in his new modern venture.

"Does a tractor-selling tycoon still attend my Louisville smoker?"

"I wouldn't miss your Derby blowout for all the tea in Taipei. A few dozen crawler sales will cover my stake."

Odell hustled back into the Georgian lobby; the bearded architect and the banjo-eyed wife tracked his path to Cotton and Arch. "Your car is here, and your bag is loaded, Mr. Carrel."

"Much obliged." Arch turned towards the front desk.

"The bugle calls."

"I'll see you at the Brown this spring. I'm wagering you'll have your stake covered and more."

"See ya' then." Cotton watched his friend leave and decided he'd head to the family farm, make a few sales calls on the way. His father would be staying in at the Dwyer house tonight, and he and his mother could enjoy a nice supper together. The only tough question he'd have to endure was when she asked if he had a steady sweetheart.

Chapter 10

Standing at the top of the landing the last night of the Edelman Brothers' visit, Molly held her cheeks high, her breasts swelling. The madam had prepared a fresh concoction for this evening's festivities, mixing in a flaky white powder she cooked in a spoon along with the vile, blue potion, and Molly was convinced she could glide down the stairs. Anticipating the madam's cue, she listened to the Edelman Brothers awaiting her entrance into the parlor. The dozen men appeared to all be kin, with their hawk noses and curly black hair, but she couldn't tell if they were brothers, cousins, or related only by commerce. They'd renamed the lodge the *Hotseplots Hotel*, and three or four times a day, one of them demanded Zach Hinton drive them into town to send a telegram or to his office to make a long-distance phone call. With strange words like *feh* and *pisher*, they cursed each other, and only one of the younger ones in the group was nice to the staff and the parlor girls. But they spent money like they could manufacture it with a cotton gin.

Molly heard the clanging of the brass gong, and Madam Mercier commenced with her speech.

"Gentlemen, gentlemen, quiet down, this is worth your attention," the madam shouted and the noise in the parlor dropped to a low din. "Tonight, one fortunate man will not only have the rare opportunity to savor a delicacy." The men howled. "But also aid an unfortunate waif." The room got quiet again. "I'm sure you've seen Molly, our tender young kitchen girl." A short whoop broke out. "Yes, she's truly an untamed beauty, but the poor child's parents were tragically swept away in the Great Tri-State Tornado leaving Molly a destitute orphan, unable to afford her lifelong dream of attending college to be a nurse. Alas, these aspirations have been ripped asunder, until this very night. For Molly has seen the virtue shining in your lion hearts and has decided that she would like one of you, the elected nobles, to lead her from maidenhood to womanhood in order to finance her ambitions. So I introduce to you the Virgin Molly."

A roar came from downstairs, and Molly began her procession. Approaching the parlor, she heard the tinkling of the piano coming from the phonograph.

Tired of being lonely, tired of bein' blue
I wish I had some good man to tell my troubles to

As Molly entered the parlor the men around the room cheered. The singer's sultry baying fueled her promenade, and she swayed her hips from side-to-side. Chasseing around the room in the ivory camisole and pettiskirt the madam had given her to wear, Molly latched onto the men's leering grins and the feigned smiles of the parlor girls sitting on their laps. She tilted her head back and paraded about the perimeter of the room again, allowing the growling vocalists to play the temptress.

Cause I need a little sugar in my bowl, doggone it
I need some sugar in my bowl

Molly stopped in the center of the room and curtsied as the madam had suggested. The crowd's fervor infused her body, and she added a wobbly shimmy she'd seen the parlor girls do. As the song ended, one of the satin straps of the camisole slipped off her shoulder and the men whooped and applauded. She pulled it back up. The raucous crowd hissed.

Madam Mercier handed her a flute of champagne, and Molly drank it down like it was cool well water.

"Boys, not much I can add to that entrance," the madam

said, refilling Molly's flute. "Highest bidder—cash on her pretty barrelhead—plucks the juicy peach from her unsullied tree. Now, in a fancy Knickerbocker knock shop, such a rare treat would cost you five thousand. But here at the Sporting Lodge, the finer things are more reasonably priced. So who'll bid two grand?"

The vigor drained from the crowd, and they stared at the madam and Molly in the center of the parlor. Hinton and Whip, dressed in their black pinstriped Sunday suits like Otto and Jacob Edelman, shifted in the corner. The shill the madam brought in, an oily man Sally called Doc Tonic, lit a cigar, his eyes twitching.

"OK, how about a thousand?"

The roomful of men remained mum.

"Five-hundred bucks?"

"I bid a nifty fifty for her," Otto Edelman, the older of the two brothers, said.

"Thank you, Mr. Otto, I've got fifty who'll give me one hundred?"

"Dig in my trousers, baby doll?" Jacob Edelman said to Viola sitting on his lap. She pulled out a wad of bills and showed it to him. "I'll bid a hundred for the virgin and sweet cheeks here, a twofer. Heaven forbid my older brother suffers a heart attack."

"I'll consider that for one hundred," the madam said. "Who's in at two-hundred for a solo with Molly?"

Tracking the madam's call for bids, Molly felt the room shrinking and she closed her eyes for a second to steady herself, realizing that the moment she'd heard about since her first night at the lodge existed beyond her thoughts. She was certain that somehow she was to blame for its creation.

"Anybody in for two?" Madam Mercier said with a jittery edge.

The nervous doubt in the madam's voice jolted Molly's gut.

"Fellas, bid, c'mon. You think I can handle a twofer?"

Jacob said, as his older brother and the others in the room doubled over in laughter.

"I'll give you two-hundred dollars," a tall man, standing in the corner, said.

Molly guessed that he, the polite one, was one of the younger men in the group. Every evening, he'd been the last one to finish his meal, and after the dining room cleared out, he'd cover his plate with his napkin, push back from the table, and cross his legs like the downtown preacher did. He'd read from his book of verses, and while she and Sally cleared the tables, he'd chat about the warm weather and the red cross-bills he'd sighted. His dark alert eyes and smoothly polished cheeks reminded her of a picture book bible version of King David. She hadn't seen him drunk, until tonight.

"Your future son-in-law is saving the firm by fucking this *shiksa*," Otto said turning to his brother, Jacob.

"With his book of clients," Jacob replied, "he's earned a night of leniency."

"Don't make this like pulling a hen's hind teeth, who's in for three hundred?" Madam Mercier signaled Doc Tonic.

Sipping more champagne, Molly looked down at the rug. It was her first time in the parlor after eight o'clock. The cigar smoke wasn't as stale as when she cleaned in the afternoon, and the voices weren't muffled by the floorboards, faceless and void of meaning. The parlor girls sat on the guest's lap, laughing carefree. They were the picnickers in the painting of the meadow that hung next to grandfather clock. Every evening, as the vibration of the gong resounded through-out the lodge, they stepped out from the bright meadow on the wall and spread their picnic to the parlor. She took another drink, trusting that the ripe bubbles would soothe her quivering stomach.

"I'm in at three," the oily doctor said, raising his hand. The entire Edelman Brothers group shifted to look at him.

"Thank you, good doctor, I've got three. How about four hundred?"

"Come on, Gabe, don't let this *schlemiel* outbid you," Jacob yelled at his future son-in-law.

"Madam Mercier, I'll bid you five-hundred dollars—cash on the pretty barrelhead," Gabe said, bringing out a brimming billfold. "But before we let the good doctor bid again, I'd like to see his cash."

"I don't think that's necessary. You are all fine fellows, outstanding gentlemen," the madam said like she was trying to swallow a forkful of Lizzy's chicken without choking on a buried bone. "I'm sure he can provide able backing."

"I say, if he can't show his dough, here's my five-hundred bucks. I'm ready to pluck a peach." Gabe came out into the center of the room and stood next to the madam and Molly. "No offense, doc."

Adjusting his shirt sleeve, Doc Tonic shuffled closer to Hinton and Whip, appearing to recede into the drapery. "None taken," he said, with a curdled expression like he'd been caught carrying in fresh manure on his boots. "I thank you for ensuring that this young girl's charms didn't carry me away."

"Anytime," Gabe said, handing the madam a five-hundred dollar bill.

The madam tucked the bill down the front of her new sequined dress.

"Wish me luck, fellas." Gabe snatched her arm, grabbed a nearly full bottle of champagne, and handed it to his new prize. Jacob Edelman led the rest of his group in a standing ovation as his future son-in-law marched Molly upstairs.

The man's grip seemed like a shackle around her wrist, and her earlier buoyancy had evaporated. Molly needed to hear the soulful song again and have the madam reassure her with a smile that another dose would be coming soon, but Madam Mercier was busy flirting with Jacob, her back turned.

"Which room is yours?" Gabe asked when they reached the landing.

Guzzling warm champagne straight from the bottle, Molly lurched down the hall, towing the winning bidder into her room.

"Lock that door." Gabe said.

Molly searched for a way to explain that she'd never been given a key to her room. Staring at the door, she spotted a skeleton key hanging on the doorknob. The quaking in her belly doubled as she fumbled with the lock. In the dimly lit room, Gabe plopped down on the side of her bed, slipping off his shoes and undoing his suspenders. Molly hesitated, lingering in her camisole. If he didn't ask to turn on the overhead light everything would be fine.

"Hell, I haven't had a private moment since we started this boondoggle." Gabe pulled out a gold metal case and lit a cigarette.

Molly gulped more champagne; she was unable to concentrate on Gabe's recount of all the places and people he's visited in the past two or three weeks. Stripping off her linen camisole, she strained to focus on the barrage of advice Sally and the parlor girls had given her. The madam compared the pain to a night of being sick, forgotten by the morning, and Molly wished that it were already a passing memory, like another group of lodge guests. Removing her pettiskirt, Molly crawled onto the bed and crouched on all fours, facing the headboard, training her thoughts on the gaps in the seams of the wallpaper. The chilly air flowed over her exposed hind end, and she clenched her ass cheeks together.

"Whoa, slow down, I'm not helping a sheep over the fence," Gabe said laughing. "You want a smoke?"

"No, thank you," Molly said, turning over onto her side, facing away from Gabe and the flavorful bite of his cologne.

"Here, you're probably freezing." Gabe slid out of bed and placed a piece of kindling onto the fire.

Slipping under the covers, Molly watched Gabe stoke the fire, curious if he'd detected her fading scars.

"I don't mind Jacob thinking I'm laying the coal to you," Gabe said, taking off his shirt and trousers before returning to bed. "But this is more about getting away from them snoring *schmucks* than plucking any peaches. I don't want any problems for my first time with Ester. We're getting married in April, traveling to Europe for our honeymoon. Going to lay a carnation on Oscar Wilde's grave. You ever been to Paris?"

"No, no, sir," Molly said, unable to imagine leaving this room tonight, much less traveling beyond Scots Station. Every evening, this bed would be her home until Jesus descended with a shout and the trumpet of God.

"You like poetry?"

Molly tried to remember the poem she'd been forced to recite in school. It had been about a captain, and Skillet had cursed the teacher when he heard her reciting it. "I love it."

"Just 'cause we aren't *shtupping*, doesn't mean we can't have little fun." Gabe rooted beneath the sheets for a minute. Gripping her hand, he tugged it to his crotch.

Molly felt like she grasping a lukewarm plate of stewed vegetables.

Gabe began a recitation. *"Houses and rooms are full of perfumes, the shelves / Are / Crowded with perfumes."* Then, "Rub on it." Tempering his pitch, he placed his hand over the top of hers, showing what he meant before drawing his hand back.

Molly squeezed his penis, yanking it hard, thinking of the strange words the parlor girls used to describe it: blind meat, Willie the worm, and one-eyed snake.

"Not like you're strangling a chicken, more like you're petting a cat."

Putting her calloused fingers across the tip, she stroked it, and as it grew harder her own blood began rushing. Molly sensed that her touch had as much control as the images Gabe was creating, and the singer's teasing plea for sugar was a ruse, like play-acting desire.

"That's it," Gabe moaned, continuing his recitation.

She worked her hand faster up and down. Beneath the sheets, it was nice and warm, and the rekindled fire loosened her body. This was easier than milking a cow that kicks, and if she switched hands, she could keep going until midnight.

Too breathless to continue his poem, Gabe pulled the covers off, slipped his dick away from her hand, and knelt next to her. Swinging his left leg across her chest, he straddled her like she was a pony at the county fair.

Drawing back from the weight of his torso, Molly scooched up to the bed towards the headboard.

Gabe pursued her. "Do they have ice cream in Alabama?" he asked, sticking his erection in her face.

"Ice cream?" she replied, glancing at the locked bedroom door. Gabe thrust his dick at her mouth. His mound of wiry pubic hair, stinking of moldy clothes, bristled against her cheeks. She turned away.

Clamping his hands around her skull, he poked his dick between her lips. "Don't be coy. Pretend you're relishing a vanilla cone."

Molly gagged as he invaded her mouth like a serpent in the garden, his spongy flesh the bitter flavor of dandelion root tea. Gabe rocked his hips in rhythm, forcing her to keep up with his back-and-forth motions. The room was now as hot as a July tobacco plot. Sweat dripped off Gabe's chest, falling onto her forehead and into her hair. She squeezed her eyes shut, wishing she was holding her breath below the surface of the lily pond, yellow flowers floating on the ceiling above her.

"Oh, that's, cripes almighty, that's, yeah." Gabe shook in a spasm.

A warm glob of liquid coated her mouth choking her. Gabe let out a heavy sigh and jerked his penis from her mouth. She gasped for air. The sticky fluid, hot and salty as boiled goobers, oozed between her lips. It had to be blood. Whip would peel her hide. The parlor girls should've warned her.

"You've made me get too excited, carried away," Gabe said, not groaning in pain. "Try a few gulps of champagne." He rolled over, his crotch not gushing.

Molly spat a murky pale clump into her palm. If wasn't his blood, then it must be his seed in her mouth. No one had told her that a man—a polite gentleman who sat in a chair like a preacher—would behave in such a way, but she should've known. Nor had they told her how to dispose of such a mess. She wiped her hand on the side of the mattress and, lifting the bedding to her mouth, spewed the bulk of the thick syrupy blob onto the sheets, grateful that Sally washed the linens. Grabbing the champagne bottle from the nightstand, she rinsed her mouth out and spewed the remnants into the chamber pot, hacking loud enough to disturb his snoring. Sinking back into the bed, she cast the stained bed sheet over Gabe and covered herself with the quilt. The wild orange reflection of the fire wavered on the walls. A harsh, briny aftertaste lingered, but now she could rest. The madam was right—no worse than heaving up a can of pickled beef tongue. It wasn't as wicked as a man spilling his seed on the ground, and it was the only means to pay her father's debt. Whatever happened next, it was sensible to court Madam Mercier's friendship. Best to be prepared, like the slave who tends the wicks and stays alert, waiting for her master's returns.

.

Chapter 11

"Hurry up, you bastards, you'll make us miss our train," a man shouted from the front of the lodge, below her bedroom window.

Molly moaned. Her skull thumped.

"And this clean country air is smelling a bit ripe this morning," the man screamed louder.

Molly considered checking on the commotion, but then she recognized the voice of Jacob Edelman. The fire was out, her belly percolated with nausea, and the creeping sunshine piled on her headache. The warmth beneath the quilt was her only comfort. She never recalled the morning light being this bright in her bedroom. Since she'd been at the lodge, Sally had woken her every morning before sunrise. She sat upright in bed. Peering around the room, there were no signs of Gabe's gold cigarette case or his trousers. The grind of the church bus gears meant that the Wall Street group was off. Flopping back, she burrowed beneath the quilt, deciphering what her delinquency would cost her. She'd missed her breakfast chores, but it was only the first time. The thin edge of what seemed like a piece of paper brushed against her face. There was a gentle rap on her bedroom door.

"*Ma chérie?*" Madam Mercier said through the door, knocking harder.

"Yes, ma'am." Molly stuck her head out from the cover and by instinct grabbed at the annoyance tickling her nose, crumpling it in her hand.

The bedroom door opened, and the madam entered. Sally trailed behind her, focused on not dropping the tray she was carrying.

"At least the crafty bastard didn't tear off your clothes."

Madam Mercier handed Molly her camisole off the floor. "Sit the tray down on the bed, Sal."

Sally stopped next to the bedside examining the sheets before she set the silver tray on Molly's lap. "You reckon I should fetch some udder cream?" She wrinkled her nose sniffing the room.

"No, that's fine, but be a lovely and get that fire going. It's colder than Eskimo cock in here," the madam said.

"I bet their willies is freezing living in them ice huts." Sally laughed and began working on the fire. "What'd that magazine call 'em?"

"Igloos." The madam picked up the napkin, tucked it into her bathrobe and examined the platter of steak and eggs with champagne and coffee. "But I imagine Ms. Lizzy don't want you up here chattering about while she's scrubbing pots and pans."

"I bet she's probably ready for a taste of Christmas," Sally said, striking a match to the kindling wood.

Madam Mercier leaned in closer to Molly, cutting a piece of flat iron steak.

"I best hurry on." Sally glanced back at the madam sitting on the edge of Molly's bed

"You best, and before you go traipsing off into the woods this afternoon don't forget to get fresh sheets on this bed."

"I bet them linens is as god-awful smelling as week old catfish heads rotting in the pit," Sally said with a grunt before shutting the door behind her and rushed downstairs.

"So?" the madam asked in between nibbles of steak.

Looking down at the silver breakfast tray, Molly traced Sally's footsteps resounding through the lodge, hurrying toward the steady calm of scrubbing the cast iron clean. "I'm sorry about missing my chores." There was a raspy morning thickness in Molly's throat.

"Don't fret that. Did you bleed?" Madam Mercier asked if she was a homey midwife.

"That's just it, ma'am."

"I'd bet you got broke hoeing black gumbo dirt."

"He didn't really do it."

"He didn't poke you?"

"No, ma'am, he just made me—" Molly paused, trying to recall the patchwork of last night.

"Made you what?"

"Sort of milk it for him, and he recited this poem about perfume and men. I couldn't figure it."

"That's as queer as a double-dick billy goat. He paid five hundred for a two-bit handy?"

"Not entirely." The sickness in her stomach was now a hard knot, and Molly wanted the tray of runny fried eggs off her lap. "He did his business in my mouth."

Madam Mercier picked up the champagne. "*Chérie*, if you only copped a doddle, you're still a virgin."

The sparkling bubbles surged to the top of the champagne flute, and Molly was pleased that each golden bead the madam swallowed made her happier. Tonight, maybe she'd give her an extra heaping dose.

"Don't you tell a soul what happened, you understand? You let them all think what they think—he had a johnson as big and hard as a lead pipe and you can hardly walk this morning."

"Yes, ma'am."

"I'd wager we could run these virgin auctions the rest of the hunting season. You'll start rolling your own dough before spring."

"Whatever you think is best," Molly said, not intending to sound like one of the parlor girls flattering lodge guests.

"Eat a bite of eggs and drink some chicory coffee," the madam said, cutting another piece of steak. "The shimmy at the end was cute, but don't overdo it." Madam Mercier washed down a bite of steak with more champagne and continued. "Sporting isn't a bad spell in the sun—as long as no fools puts it where it don't belong. Some tip, most don't, but if you pinch a few bucks, only take a morsel and not a whole slice." The madam finished the last of the champagne. "Most of these whiskey dicks are insults to pleasure making. Yet every other blue moon a beau comes along that makes your eyes swim around and your insides juicy and bursting like a bucket of wild blackberries. Watch out where those types can take your mind."

Molly tucked her hand holding the crumpled note further under the spread, squeezing it tight; there was a soft graininess to it like the bills Alma Mae doled out for her to go pay the grocery chit, treating each threadbare dollar like it contained all of Samson's strength. If charming drunken lechers into paying her hefty tips was her route to freedom, Molly supposed she could learn to play Delilah among the parlor girls. "Sorry, I don't know what happened with my breakfast chores this morning."

"I said don't fret about it," the madam said, standing up to leave. "This afternoon you can go with Sally to chop us down a *Noël* tree. Let her tell you what she wants from old Saint Nick."

The bedroom door clicked shut, and Molly waited, counting to ten before she pulled her hand out from the spread, discovering a timeworn twenty in her palm. Molly was certain she'd seen the dour old man on one side of the bill at the lodge, but the other side, with its engraved locomotive and steamship, stirred a notion within her. Like the parlor girls and the meadow painting, she wished she could vanish into the train's passenger car or the deck of the ocean liner, the inky smoke rising from the stacks and fading into the cityscape. With a smiling blue-eyed beau holding her close, a dapper fellow in a cashmere topcoat and fedora who made her swoon, she would peer over the rail and watch the steamer slice through the rising swells. She slipped her new fortune under her mattress, hiding it in a torn opening in the fabric. If Alma Mae did show up Christmas morning with a fat pot-of-gold and begging her with a sack of gifts, Molly was staying with Madam Mercier. And by the time the dogwoods bloomed, she'd be someplace far better than Scots Station.

Chapter 12

Out the back door of the cookhouse, a path led away from the lodge into the woods. After fifty or sixty paces it split at the withered red oak, the left fork heading to the Watts' place and the right fork veering off toward the old mill and Sally's cottage. Later that afternoon, while Madam Mercier rested and the parlor girls styled one another's hair while they drank corn liquor, Molly and Sally walked down the narrow rutted path to the cottage; it was the first time Molly had ever ventured out behind the lodge.

"I'm pretty sure I used the ax last week," Sally said, staying a few steps ahead. "And the bow saw was lying next to my woodpile, I do believe."

The brisk pace and the outdoor air were clearing her mind, and her headache had gone from a thump to a dull thud. Her stomach had settled down, but she was eager to chop down the tree and return to the lodge before Sally got them lost in the dense woods after dark.

Not far after the fork, they came to the remains of the mill's stone foundation and the scaffolding that carried the waterwheel. Set off on the edge of the tree line was Sally's cottage. They scurried across the mill's tottering footbridge, leading over the dried-up stream, and Sally ran to the slumping woodpile next to the porch. The bleached-out cottage had the same skewed appearance as the Lingo's shack, and if it had been adjacent to a cotton field or a tobacco plat rather than an old mill, it would've been called a tenant house, not a cottage. Hanging off the front porch were a series of gourds with the painted faces of demons, and amidst the sharp teeth and glowering red eyes of the masked gourds were the carcasses of small animals: black squirrels, blue jays, and an orange tabby cat, dangling like executed criminals. The buzzing flies and rotting stench sent Molly's stomach churning again.

"See, they was right where I left them. Here, you take the saw, and I'll carry the ax." Sally thrust the rusty bow saw in Molly's direction, but she stood stiff, staring at the cottage's trimmings. The plump redhead extended the saw again, bumping it against Molly's hip. "You ain't gonna make me lug both."

"Sorry," Molly said, grabbing the saw's slender long handle. She turned away from the cottage and studied the collection of fieldstones that once supported the grinding plant.

"They're my totems. I found 'em dead already," Sally said loud enough to draw Molly's attention back to the unnatural adornments. "Lizzy says they're sorcery, but Bucktooth Becky told me to put 'em up before she left to go back to Baton Rouge. She says, they'd protect me from all the wickedness lurking in these woods. You gotta trust in something, don't you?"

"I suppose so," Molly said, cutting her short like a school marm with a frustrating student.

"I'd wager so, like the Holy Bible," Sally said, tossing the ax over her shoulder. "I seem to remember a little patch of Scot Pines not too far away." She marched off to the tree line, and Molly followed behind.

Tromping through the woods, Sally prattled on about every Christmas she could remember and how she had heard Madam Mercier convincing Hinton to give them a radio as a present. Molly trudged after her focusing her thoughts on the twenty-dollar bill tucked into her mattress, picturing herself drinking afternoon tea and eating finger sandwiches in one of those white marble New York hotels she'd read about in *Ragged Dick*. They weaved around briar thickets and over moss-covered logs until Sally was out of breath and Molly was worn thin searching for any resemblance of a Christmas tree. Finally, they came across an open patch and a line of evergreens that had served as a windbreak to a razed house, of which only a crumbling chimney was still standing.

"See, like I told you," Sally said, standing in front of the row of hearty evergreens. "I say we go for that one there." She pointed to the tallest and widest one in the string. "That'll fill up the front room."

"I was thinking more that one." Molly stepped toward the smallest one at the end of the line. "Them others are too big for us to get back."

"Not me, besides, I'd round up Mr. Isaiah and his boys to help haul it back in the wagon, if we needed it," Sally said, rushing to her tree.

"Nah, we don't want to be bothering them. Anyways, Madam Mercier told me she likes a tree short enough for her to put the angel on the top all by herself."

"What angel?"

"I don't know, might be a surprise." Molly said, suppressing the fatigue seeping through her back and legs. Practicing her syrupy parlor girl voice, she walked near Sally. "I like your tree fine, but I'm worried about us making the madam happy. You can take credit if you like."

"If you like it, you chop it." Sally plopped the ax down at Molly's feet.

Molly snatched the ax up off the ground. "It isn't the first tree I chopped down with other folks standing around," she said, stalking back to the small pine. With each swing of the blunt blade, Molly breathed silent swears at Sally with the same vengeance she would've had toward her mother, and with the tree near ready to fall, she tossed down the useless ax and kicked at the tree until it toppled onto its side. Picking up the pruning saw, she trimmed off the jagged bottom and glared at Sally standing there with her arms crossed and hip poked out to the side. She brushed the shavings off her dress. "You aren't making me tell the madam you made me tote it, too."

"I'm taking a shortcut back," Sally said, hoisting up the base of the tree.

Molly watched Sally slog away with the tree in tow, but

her legs were too weary to follow. She was left alone with the decaying chimney, its blood-red bricks blanched pale by the years. Daydreaming that the deserted household could be resurrected, she dropped her arms to her side. In her mind, she rebuilt a genuine cottage with clapboards painted the light purple of wisteria vines and gingerbread house trim curving along the front porch. Skillet returned, clean-shaven and sober, full of road tales and his plans for restoring the old mill. Alma Mae's father sent her back with Stanley and made her vow to be a God-fearing wife like she was raised to be. Water flowed under the fieldstones and the mill wheel turned again. Tenant farmers came to them, bringing them more business than any ledger could hold. She deserved it. She said her prayers in secret and put her nickel in the wicker basket most every Sunday. She'd endured the madam's auction scheme and the lustful stares of the strangers. She'd read her Bible stories—what she wanted was a pittance to the Almighty, a mere trifling, like Gabe's twenty-dollar tip for jamming it in her mouth.

A red fox slinked out from the dark opening of the chimney's firebox, stopping to fix its squinty gaze on Molly. She formed two fists and searched for a big stick or a rock in case the scruffy creature came her way. The Lord had filled these woods with beasts, big and small, at the time of the Garden of Eden, and long after she'd returned to dust, wild animals and their spirits would inhabit the land. With a swish of its bushy white tail, it chased after a woodrat or a rabbit, only it could hear rustling in the woods. Sally had long disappeared, and Molly's craving stirred for her nightly potions and her hidden money. "I'm coming, Sal, hold up."

Molly hurried after her, but when she caught up, Sally didn't bother to turn around. She picked up the trailing end of the tree, the evergreen's gummy pine tar coating her hands. They carried it in tandem, neither speaking, down a steep incline into a gulch, where the girls stopped to rest. A sulfur stench, more putrid than Sally's rotting totems, burned

Molly's nostrils.

"What's that awful smell?" Molly covered her nose with the crook of her elbow.

"That'd be the pit," Sally said, pointing to the far end of the gulch.

Unmasking her face, Molly took a reluctant step toward the pile of charred logs and stones, and a claw reached up from the burnt opening and grabbed hold of her, dragging her closer. She stopped along the edge. She knew the shallow burn pit was used to incinerate the rubbish from the lodge, leftover hog and chicken renderings from the cookhouse mainly. But peering down into the scorched hole, she felt a tightening in her chest. The invisible claw squeezed the air from her lungs.

"I was out hunting root that night, right up on the ridge." Sally said, skulking up next to Molly. "I seen what they did to that man."

Molly locked on Sally's face, pressing herself to understand the glint of delight in her voice.

"I heard 'em coming, all of 'em whooping and hollering. I wanted to find me some queen root and fix my spell, attract me a pretty man, so I hid out behind that stunted tree up there. He wasn't hardly moving when they cut him loose from the rail."

Closing her eyes, Molly listened to rest of Sally's story.

"But when they doused him with kerosene and lit him up, he screamed and twisted until his last breath like a wild beast. Then they kicked him into the pit and threw more fuel on him, started a big old bonfire, flames soaring as high as the treetops. I could see all of 'em, passing their jug, pulling out their tallywhackers, and pissing into the pit."

With her eyes sealed shut, a photograph sprouted from the front of her skull, a vision of her father and a woman appearing in her mind.

"I'm heading to the lodge to show Madam Mercier this tree I fetched for her."

Sally's voice trailed off, and Molly concentrated on the

ethereal image of her father and the woman standing next to him, the young brown-haired woman, who'd warned her about the black-hearted angels. She'd been in every season of her life. Not caring about the madam, her potions, or her money, she sensed they needed to speak to her, revealing a secret that only she was supposed to know, but the vision faded like a dream sworn to be remembered, vanishing with the memories of her father's scratchy cheeks or his wild laughter at his own stories.

The electric lights of the lodge were scarcely visible through the dusky silhouette of trees. Not seeking the path, Molly stumbled between the clumps of barren hardwoods and pines. She could have allowed Hinton to take her that night. She could have been Pug and the Deacon's whore. Her father would be still alive, and she'd have a common bond with her mother, but the chance to strike that crooked bargain was buried in the pit. The back of her dress was drenched in sweat as she fought her way through the thicket. After she soaked in a hot tub, she might let one of the parlor girls paint her nails, maybe like the photo spreads in the *Broadway Brevities* magazine. She'd show Hinton what a good servant she'd become. She'd wait, and as she heard Deacon Conyers say in Sunday school, "the foot of the unrighteous will slip and the Lord's people will have their retribution." Her sword would devour Mr. Zach's flabby flesh and become drunk with his blood.

Subscribe to Southern Fried Karma's YouTube channel, Fugitive Views, to hear about impact of religion and superstition on Molly's life.

Chapter 13

By mid-morning, the St. George train depot, not much larger than the entrance hall at Creekside, was packed with holiday travelers. Hayseed families, shovel-headed fathers and round-faced mothers with three or four crusty-nosed jackanapes, headed east to visit their Polack kin in Chicago or north to see Sven and Ole in Minnesota. There was little room for walking around, and the only place that made Cotton feel like he wasn't being stared at was in the corner next to a darkie by himself.

Leaning against the rough brick wall, Cotton pulled his scarf up over his nose and mouth. The potbelly stove and the throng of stranded passengers kept the room plenty warm, but there was enough hacking and wheezing in the cramped waiting room to provoke an influenza epidemic. He wanted the only Christmas gift he brought home his mother to be the small ceramic figurine he purchased in St. Louis and not a pestilent virus. He reached inside his coat pocket for his pint bottle, but remembered he'd finished it last night, celebrating alone in his hotel room. The stern Norwegian engineers had abstained and the chambermaid wasn't a candidate. She had a wooden leg—lost it when her sodden grandpa had clipped her with the steel-toothed mower. Despite her sunny congeniality and sonsy curves, Cotton wasn't prepared to deviate into the sideshow realm.

Cotton patted his other coat pocket. The thick manila envelope was still there. He'd signed a contract with the Hansen Tractor Company. James Wakeman, his father's business partner, had confirmed Odom's story. The legislature had approved funding for a new state highway system, and Brewer held sole power over the final plans and the construction equipment. Wakeman had given Cotton permission to contact the list of manufacturers Archie had provided, but not to sneak away to Iowa the weekend before the holiday shutdown. Nor to sign a contract for Southeastern distribution rights. Nor to use a thousand-dollar loan from his mother as a deposit to order three crawlers. But when he landed the State deal before the first demonstrator was delivered in the spring, he knew no challenges would be made.

Gnawing on the ragged nub of his fingernail, he studied the train schedule for the umpteenth time. An Alberta Clipper had blown through a few days ago, blanketing the Plains with over a foot of snow, and the hard, gray skies hadn't changed since Cotton's arrival. According to the ill-tempered clerk, all the trains from St. Louis were postponed until tomorrow, the Illinois Central to Chicago was still delayed and had been for days, and Cotton couldn't figure how going north to St. Paul could help him get south to Georgia. His mother had only made one extempore stipulation before advancing the funds to her son. A family holiday at Creekside was all the collateral she required: stringing popcorn on the tree, lighting the Advent candles on Christmas Eve. He flicked through the small print pages of the schedule without reading them.

"Where you heading?" the darkie asked.

"Atlanta, or thereabouts," Cotton replied. For a traveling negro, he was well-dressed in a gray herringbone suit and light-colored spats. His thick hair was flattened with a slight wave. With a quick tug, he could tighten up his loose paisley necktie and be as dapper as any gentleman Cotton knew. He was sitting on top of a haggard leather valise, and a short rectangular hard case was next to him, protected between him and the wall. "You?"

"New Orleans, or thereabouts." The stranger sipped from a flask. He extended it to Cotton. "Anywhere but here."

Cotton glanced at the booking clerk behind the counter, then down at the tarnished flask. "A might bit early." The man's manicured fingers were long and lustrous, not those of a laborer, rather someone who treated his hands with caution, like precise instruments.

The black stranger raised the dented silver bottle closer.

Taking the flask from the stranger's delicate hand, Cotton gulped down a nice swallow. It wasn't Huck's shine, but it had the proper blend of bite and thirst quencher. He handed it back. "Obliged."

"You waiting for the Memphis MidAmerican?" The stranger tucked the flask into the side pocket of his suit coat.

"Nah, I didn't see it listed in the schedule."

"That's cause it's a special route."

"Special?" Cotton asked, wondering how the stranger could know more about the train schedule than the crabby booking clerk.

"Mainly taking colored folks home to visit relations. You'll need to inquire at the counter."

"Sure enough?"

"Sure enough, it'll get you to Memphis, where you can get anywhere worth getting."

Cotton picked up his grip. "Obliged again," he said with a two-fingered salute. The stranger dipped his head and smiled. Once they got to Memphis, he'd buy them a bottle of bootleg hooch at the taxi stand. He'd find out how it was that a dapper darkie landed in the middle of hog-slop Iowa with a cryptic train schedule.

At Memphis Central Station, he could catch the Crescent overnight to West Point. He'd be home in time to ensure there was adequate rum in Adah's eggnog and not taint his mother's Christmas. Being absent, or tardy, would increase the odds of Mr. Arnold becoming aware of her private investment. He'd have her paid back before his father was the wiser—all he needed was to get Brewer to the lodge for a weekend. The whiskey and the whores could tackle any work the Hansen crawler couldn't.

Chapter 14

Christmas at the Sporting Lodge consisted of Sally burning every meal while waiting for Hinton to deliver their new radio, Madam Mercier worrying about her supply of potion, and Viola and Pearl promising Molly that their tongues could make her feel better than Rudolph Valentino if he'd still been alive. Alma Mae didn't show up with a bag full of presents, and any scrap of holiday cheer was forgotten when a new group of guests, door-to-door sales contest winners, arrived before New Year's.

The oafish contest winners, like all the lodge guests that followed that hunting season, weren't as savvy bidders as the Edelman Brothers group, or as free with their cash, and the winners weren't satisfied with a poem and her mouth copping their doddle. Each week, as the guests' prey switched from whitetail deer to pintail ducks to bobwhite quail, Molly would spend the first two or three days playing the role of the innocent kitchen girl, and the final night they'd reprise the virgin auction. Doc Tonic didn't come around again, but Madam Mercier improved at pulling ghost bids from the crowd. With her reserve of vials dwindling low, the madam only set aside a dose for Molly on auction nights, and allowed her a jug of Hinton's homebrew to drink before she paraded into the parlor, always accompanied by "I Need a Little Sugar in My Bowl." Molly saw her own promenade of peckers: tiny peters shorter than her middle finger, uncircumcised ones like ears of unhusked corn growing in an overgrown patch of wiry hair, and the most recent one that was as large as a cucumber. None of them produced a rush of maddening pleasure; merely a hint that it might be possible for a man and his unruly appendage to be more than a temporary irritant between her legs and a wallet to pick a few bills from after they passed out.

When the Bradford pear trees in front of the lodge unleashed the sour bloom of spring, Molly had abandoned any notion that her mother would return. She endured the auction evenings in a trance, passing the night by tracking the serpentine pattern in the tattered carpet lining the stairs.

The hunting groups were smaller late in the season, filling up the lodge with awkward pairings like automobile dealers and undergarment manufacturers. Yet one group's impending visit had Madam Mercier asking almost hourly if the "nosy old-timer" had delivered a telegram confirming their arrival date. Finally, on the sunniest afternoon of the year, the madam's telegram arrived, and Molly carried it to her on the sun porch.

Madam Mercier ripped open the envelope and scanned the message. "We need to scrounge up two or three bottles of real whiskey, Scotch would be best," the madam said, pushing herself up from the lounge. "Then we'll need to clean the far north guest rooms, the two large ones, extra thorough." She read the telegram again and smiled. "Go fetch my *Fannie Farmer* off my desk. Ms. Lizzy has gotta cook a dinner fancier than her fried yard bird." She handed Molly the bedroom key from her wrist clutch. "I wonder if it's too late to order a crate of beefsteaks. Leave the key over the door just in case."

"Yes, ma'am," Molly said, imagining the type of red-blooded man that could generate such eagerness. Sashaying around the leather chaise, Madam Mercier studied the telegram once more, not looking up as Molly left the room, infused with a similar strut.

Scanning the desktop, Molly found the cookbook underneath a stack of mail, and she grabbed it up, preparing to hurry to the cookhouse in case Sally got too far underfoot or Ms. Lizzy got too testy, but the madam's accounting ledger was opened up in the center of the desk. Molly looked at the exposed page. Emma was written at the top left corner of the page, and dates and descriptions ran the length of the page with figures scribbled next to each entry. She sat down in the madam's chair and examined the leather-bound ledger's sums, flipping the pages until she discovered her name handwritten in a tight cursive. The first entry was for five-hundred dollars, and it was marked Lingo Family Debt. The left column listed entries for room, board, and medicine, and the right column was her wages. She was charged a dollar twenty for each of her nightly doses and earned ten dollars a week as a kitchen girl. The only amounts lowering her debt started the night of the first auction when she was given a fifty-dollar reduction, but the sums for each auction were progressively smaller. For braving that hick with the frightful carnation-pink cucumber last week, she'd only earned five dollars, after it burned her cooch and left bloody spots on the sheets. At the bottom of the page, the balance remaining was three-hundred-and-eighty-five dollars. She stood up. Calculating her path to freedom, she was baffled about who was making the most of her time in the lodge. She twirled the ribbon carrying the madam's bedroom key around her finger. Madam Mercier's satchel with her electric blue vials was stashed in the room somewhere. Like she'd been told, she'd put the key over the door, but she'd damn well earned a free share this evening.

After complaining of a headache and retiring early, Molly sat on her bedroom floor in the dark listening to the lodge. The same as the woods, the sounds and movement of houses and their inhabitants ran in patterns. She heard the crashes of laughter from the husbands and fathers teeming with lust and extra cash in a parlor full of greedy bored girls. The laughter would lead to deadened voices in the hallway as the fugitive couples ventured the forty paces upstairs. Then the voices would become guilty thrusting grunts, and the parlor girls would mark the time by hiking their backsides in the air, burying their pale faces, ignorant of any joy in the laughter and the grunts.

Madam Mercier was probably downstairs overseeing the poker game, prodding the players, the tight-fisted and the shy, to partake in "the other sport you know you can't get back home." The madam would've already taken her evening dose, and Molly knew now was the best time for her to get hers. She took a long sip of corn liquor from her crystal goblet and got up.

Cracking her door, Molly listened for any creaks on the stairs. Squeaky bed springs were the only report back. She crept down the hall, took down the waiting key, and eased the madam's bedroom door open, her trembling legs recovering when she found it empty. The madam must've treated herself well that evening, her violet satchel was still on her bed. Molly only intended to take the box with the syringe and the vials. Rummaging through the bottles in the bag, she searched for the silver box, but it wasn't there. The clomping sound of Sally running up the stairs sent the tremors coursing back through her legs.

Spotting the rectangular silver box on the nightstand, she snatched it up, tossed it in the satchel, and hurried for the door, but Sally flew into the room before she reached it. The two girls stared at one another.

"What are you doing up here?" Molly asked, summoning the gumption of every hypocrite she'd ever seen at a tent revival.

"The madam sent me for some stomach medicine." Sally pointed at the satchel in Molly's hand. "Why you here?"

"I'm bringing the madam her bag."

"Ain't you in bed with your 'right awful headache?' How'd you know what she wanted?"

"You'd be right awful surprised at what I can hear and what I know."

Sally stepped back. "I know you're a lying, thieving fornicator," she said, launching herself at the bag.

The bag fell from Molly's grip, and the girls dropped to

the floor after it. They pulled hair and pinched each other, wrestling in a circle up next to the madam's bedpost. Molly swung a leg around Sally's back and rolled her hips over, pinning her to the floor.

"Take the bag, you redheaded toad." Molly fought to press Sally's wrist to the floor. "But if you've ever say anything to Madam Mercier, I'll cast a spell on you. You'll wind up marrying some half-wit coon who'll only drop his drawers to beat you with his rope belt."

Sally wiggled her arm free, grabbed the side of Molly's head, and banged her skull into the mahogany bedpost.

Molly crumpled over, and in a blur she saw the heels of Sally's boots scurrying out of the room. She crawled down the hall to her bedroom, locked the door, and considered what she might use as a barricade. She heard sounds coming up the stairs and pushed her back to the door.

A deep burst of laughter followed by a nasal titter let her know it was Emma bringing a man upstairs, but next time it might be Madam Mercier with Whip. Turning on the overhead light, she grabbed the fire poker and searched for a small weapon that she could conceal close to her and gouge out an eye. There was nothing in her chest of drawers. She could smash the wash basin and use a shard of porcelain, but she'd rather have that as a shield. She opened the nightstand drawer, hoping Bucktooth Becky had left behind a pair of scissors or a dagger. The only thing laying inside was a small bag. It was soiled with a thin film of dried mud, but she recognized it as the pouch Alma Mae had given her the day Hinton had taken her away.

Sitting down the fire poker, she untied the velveteen pouch, and a locket, the size of a quarter, fell into her palm. It was tarnished rose gold with a rhinestone crescent moon and shining star on the front hanging from a slender chain. She unfastened the clasp, and in the photo window was a picture of a young woman. The portrait was faded and cracked in spots. *"My Lovely Rose"* was engraved on the interior of the front cover. The woman in the photograph didn't appear to be much older than Molly, and she had the same dark eyes and oval face as hers. Her braided ponytail was draped around her high lace collar, and her chin was tilted up, exposing her slender neck.

There was more laughter in the hallway, and Molly clenched the locket in her fist. She picked up her fire poker again, weighing it in her hand. It seemed like it would protect her, unless Whip grabbed hold of her or Madam Mercier pulled out her derringer. *Sleep is your weapon,* a voice said to her. Glancing around the room, Molly put the poker back down and felt for a knot on her skull muddling her mind. There was a tender spot, but her noggin wasn't busted.

From the base of her skull, the voice, soft and steady, spoke again, *sleep is your shield.* Molly shook her head, expecting the motion to clear her thoughts like wiping a grimy window clean. If Madam Mercier found her asleep in bed, Molly could claim that Sally was lying, making up tall tales because she was jealous. Nothing was missing from the madam's bedroom or her satchel, and the next auction was coming up soon. Life in the lodge had taught that her that deceiving people was easier when believing in the ruse suited their needs. They asked to be suckers. Slipping the locket around her neck, she turned out the overhead light and got in bed.

The lodge returned to its familiar nighttime pattern, and Molly counted each breath in and out, until the haze of sleep settled over her. Her mind journeyed through the nightly maze of dreams, fragmented scenes of slapping Alma Mae across the face, wading in a shallow creek with Stanley, finally arriving in a crowd of blonde town girls and pale parlor girls in straw hats with ribbons and ostrich feathers. The breeze flapped at their long Sunday dresses.

The young brown-haired woman, Rose, put her hand on Molly's shoulder.

Next, the two of them were in a field of violet meadow flowers. A river rippled past, a fleeting echo. A slight man framed in bib overalls, faded blue as the sky, rowed to the other shore. He put down his oars and flapped both hands over his head.

Rose waved back and the traveler continued crossing to the far shore.

And they were on the edge of the pit in the woods behind the lodge, flames soaring to the branches overhead. Rose tossed a ledger into the burning blaze. Watching the red-leather binding tumble end-over-end, the pages fanning out, Molly understood the Lord was not a Savior who plucked us from our troubles—he was a Refiner, purifying sinners through their suffering.

Chapter 15

Cotton loved the cards he was holding—three kings—but everyone else at the poker table made his jaw ache. The local boss man, Jack or Zach something, was a real rube, crowing so much about his hand that he had to be an imbecile, busted, or both. Corley Brewer was dead money, and Cotton had hated the jug-eared bastard across the table ever since he'd seen him play bush league ball in Augusta. He didn't give a damn about retired legends and all-time records. Muff an easy fly-ball because you were tipping your cap to a hatchet-faced farmer's daughter in the stands and you were never pardoned, twenty plus years ago or not. Making it worse, jug-ears was fishing for a flush. He watched the busty madam saunter into the smoky poker room.

"Mr. Brewer, Captain Arnold, pleasure to see you again," she said. "Everybody playing nice in here, Whip?"

The massive man standing by the window neck drooped like he was falling asleep.

On his second trip to the Sporting Lodge, Cotton had decided that the joint had the same guttural moans and fried food funk as every knock shop he'd visited from Paris to Paraguay. The Lupanar of Pompeii probably had buxom broads and bruisers like these two. Madam Mercier was devious enough to let the crowing rube think he controlled the rollicking brothel, but her jittery eyes and clammy skin proved she wasn't nearly as clever as she believed. The mute bruiser only understood what he could wrap his hands around.

The madam cozied up next to jug-ears and put her hand on the back of his chair. "Mr. Tyrus, I trust you enjoyed the Providence Chicken?"

"I'm sure it was the fanciest stewed yard bird he's ever

eaten," the rube said. "Right now, he's enjoying taking our money. Like he ain't got enough of his own. You own as much Coca-Cola stock as I hear say?"

The only reply was a glare from them both.

"I believe it's your bet, Corley," Cotton said, scheming how to keep jug-ears at the table before the rube asked another rude question, like did your mother really shoot your father as he crawled in the bedroom window? Every daily sports page had stories about him punching annoying fans in the face without ever saying a word.

Scratching his pitted flabby cheek, Corley Brewer studied his cards like building plans drawn using foreign shapes. "What's the bet?"

"A buck," Cotton said, noticing the madam's hand slip from the back of the chair to jug-ears' shoulder.

"I'm in," Brewer said, double-clutching his chip before he tossed it in the center of the green felt table.

Not glancing at his cards, Cotton matched the bet. He would've preferred Brewer had gone ahead and folded, but five or six shots of the rube's moonshine must have stoked his courage. Cotton knew the rube wanted the Alabama Public Roads Superintendent to route the highway through Scots Station and a generous tract of his bottomland, and they each needed him more than a pot in a poker game. Corley was worth fifty new crawler tractors. Getting him here had been simple. The flabby bureaucrat hunted at the lodge once or twice every season; however, the Hansen Tractor Company was late delivering the first demonstrator. The correspondence from the Norwegian engineers was getting more evasive with explanations of drive shaft hardness and supplier issues. Cotton hadn't thought to see one of their tractors running. His trip to Iowa occurred in the middle of a damnable blizzard, and he was fortunate enough to survive his Memphis bender with the cornet player. He'd caught the last Crescent to arrive home in time for the hanging of the greens.

"We got a real high-stakes contest going on later," the madam said. "One gentleman will be plucking the peach from our virgin kitchen girl this evening."

"I'd pluck that peach myself," the rube said, "but I'll have to be satisfied losing to the 'Georgia Peach' instead." He threw one chip into the pot and then another.

Jug-ears flipped two chips in the game, sneering at the other players.

"That girl's got her a juicy rump. I'd sure like to bulldoze me a road through it," Brewer said, his cards trembling.

The only kitchen girl Cotton had noticed on his trip with Odom resembled a mound of pumpkins with tangerine straw on top, but he wasn't questioning what blew the breeze in Brewer's britches. The pulsing pain surged through his jawbone. "Corley, you in for another buck?"

"How much you expecting she'll be going for?" Brewer plopped his cards down on the t-ble.

"All depends," the madam said. "Down in Mobile, or at a grand salon over in Storyville, temptations as sweet her sell for a grand or two."

"Storyville?" Brewer poked out his lips like a pair of fleshy pink spareribs. He slid his cards to the middle of the table. "I ain't seen anything around here like New Orleans boast, or Mobile for that matter. And Scots Station won't amount to a speck in a blind man's eye if it don't get it a modern highway."

"Boss man, I'll call your dollar and raise it ten," Cotton said, pushing a stack of chips into the pot.

"Don't fret now, Superintendent Brewer, we're just ginning up for the evening," the rube laughed. He chucked ten more chips into the pile.

Jug-ears eyed Cotton like he was a greenhorn pitcher who'd thrown a fastball at his chin. "I'll call that." He slung his bet onto the growing pile of chips.

"And three wise men came from the East," Cotton said, showing his cards. He figured there was enough cash in the pot to stake him in the Louisville game.

"That beats my pairs of bullets and dimes." The rube slumped back in his chair.

"How about you, Mr. Peach?" Cotton asked.

"Mr. Cobb could wipe his fanny with your ten dollars, jackass." Flinging his cards down, jug-ears stood up from the table. "I'm going to find Tommy. I'd wager he's never had an at-bat with a virgin." He stalked out of the room.

"Time for me to go check on our girl," the madam said, following behind the retired legend.

"Mr. Corley, what say I cash out and see if virgins are selling for higher than a good tractor-drawn grader? We got time for more cards later." Cotton raked his winnings into his wide-beamed trilby hat. He was certain Cobb would want another crack at the poker table. Jug-eared bastards were always looking for a fight.

Subscribe to Southern Fried Karma's YouTube channel, Fugitive Views, to hear about Ty Cobb the baseball legend and Southern icon.

Chapter 16

Molly adjusted the wick on her bedside lamp, lifted the globe off, and placed the spoon over the flame.

"The man could wipe his fanny with ten-dollar bills. You'd think losing at poker wouldn't make him rather fight than fuck," Madam Mercier said, twisting the fringe of her hemline, then smoothing it out. "Move it back and forth, it heats up faster that way."

"Yes, ma'am." Molly glided the silver teaspoon over the flame. A brownish-gold streak of smoke seeped off as the flakes begin to bubble.

"Charlie? What kind of wife name is that? Backward cunt stays knocked up. Keeps her claws in him."

The powdery flakes foamed over the heat, dissolving into a chief ingredient of the potion.

"Lying two-faced bastard. The goddamn 'Georgia Peach' can't move." The madam dabbed the sweat off her forehead. "We should tour the California coast this summer, see the sights."

"I'd like to see the sights." Molly loaded a share of the simmering liquid from the scalded teaspoon into the syringe.

"I told that Sal about laundering your camisole." The fine linen camisole was wilted from Sally boiling it and wringing it out like an ornery hen's neck.

"Careful ain't her calling," Molly said.

"It'll do. Don't want rumor spreading we sold the same virgin a dozen times," Madam Mercier said, laughing. "My dose about ready?"

Joining the madam's laughter, Molly topped off the syringe with a measure from the blue vial, saving the largest portion of each ingredient for herself. If Rose weren't merely a knock on the noggin mocking her prayers, she'd return, and a good dose could invite her arrival. "Yes, ma'am, as ready as the midnight train to Memphis."

"All aboard." Madam Mercier turned around, tugged up her dress, and grabbed the back of the chair, thrusting her buttock toward Molly. "One of the fellas from the poker room is pretty keen himself, jazzy double-breasted suit, and slicked-back blonde hair. His eyes are different, sort of green, or maybe gray."

Pausing, Molly searched between the pimply red blotches for an unbruised spot to insert the syringe.

"C'mon, girl, don't make momma beg for it," Madam Mercier said, shimmying her ass.

"Hold still." Jabbing the needle deep into a patch as blue as new denim, Molly pushed down the plunger, ignoring the madam's flinches. She pulled down the beaded dress, easing her back into the chair.

Madam Mercier purred her gratitude.

If she went on the madam's summer trip, Molly could stroll right out the front door with Sally toting her bags and Whip driving them to the station in Hinton's blue coffin-sedan. Then in St. Louis or Topeka, any city or town with boarding houses on wide paved streets, she could slip away, passing for a preacher's fiancée or a schoolmarm on her way to her new post. She fixed her dose, heftier than the madam's, hoping tonight's high-bidder would be the two-grunts-pass-out type of man. Dragging the tip of the needle along the tender underside of her arm, Molly pumped her fist, opening herself up to the auction potion. The vein in the crook of her arm bulged, and she stuck the needle in and drew back blood into the syringe, the red stream infusing with the venom. Steadily, she injected the full dose, remembering to pull the needle out before she rolled back onto the bed. With half-closed eyes, she rubbed her father's locket between her fingers. Basking in the elixir's hum, her mind called out through the vapors for her long-past grandmother, asking her to point out the proper path.

Chapter 17

After the brass gong sounded, later than was customary, Cotton and Corley joined the group of roofing manufacturers and took a spot in the dank parlor across from Cobb, Tommy, jug-ears' baseball pal, and the rube. The mute bruiser watched again from the cover of the corner, attempting to blend in with the tattered draperies.

"Gentlemen, I introduce the Virgin Molly," the glassy-eyed and swaying madam said, ending her rambling preamble to the auction. She dropped the needle on the Victrola, and a warped Bessie Smith record began crackling from the phonograph.

The kitchen girl teetered through the threshold, and Corley rocked back and forth in his chair while Cobb nudged his buddy. Cotton straightened up in his chair; it wasn't the pumpkin gal. If he'd seen a girl like this before, it had never been in a hunting lodge full of homely whores. Her bloomers looked like a pair of furrowed long-johns, but her face was as sweet as the new girl in church, fresh from being dipped in the river and born anew. Corley Brewer smacked his thick lips and rocked faster.

The song ended and the virgin kitchen girl joined the madam in the center of the room.

"Who's in for a hundred?" the madam said.

Corley Brewer's hand shot up. "I'm in her for ten dollars."

"I'll take that bid for a start, but I'm not sure that'll get you in her. Who'll give me twenty? How about you, Mr. Albertson? Any of your fellas like to lay your slates to Molly?"

The leader of the roofing group's jowly face flushed, and he shook his head.

Cobb nudged his buddy again.

Tommy cleared his throat and raised his hand. "Twenty, right over here," he said in a dull voice, like he'd been hit in the head with too many beanballs.

"I appreciate your twenty, Mr. Tommy. Who'll give me thirty?"

"By God, I'll bid thirty dollars," Corley said, his eyes blinking madly.

If Corley won the virgin, it would clear him to pick Cobb and the boss man clean at the poker table, insuring his stake for Arch's Louisville game and covering him until he closed the big sale to the State. Listing from side to side, the kitchen girl coughed and stared at the washed-out painting next to the clock. Her lips were the rich red of Italian grapes. In Alabama, or any other part of the world, Cotton should have passed her on the side of a meager country road, standing on a dilapidated porch, clinging to her momma's dress. Her only ambition should be to marry a peckerwood boy, not hook drunk lechers, so that in two or three years when Cotton traveled that same rutted path again, she'd have one or two of her own young'uns clutching her bruised thighs.

"Now we're cooking. How about forty?"

Leaning over, Cobb whispered to his buddy.

Tommy threw up his hand. "How about fifty?"

"Fifty is wonderful," the madam said.

"The call was for forty. You can't make no fifty-dollar bid," Corley said, grousing like a spoiled child at the county fair. "Ain't you got no kinda damn no rules? Protocols?"

Cotton could hear the fiery wheezing coming from Brewer's splayed nostrils. Instead of being known as the salesman that saw the Alabama Public Roads Superintendent win the virgin, he was going to be the jackass that saw him embarrassed.

"Fella, the protocol where I come from is high bid wins," Cobb said with the tone of a ruler's edict rather than that of a guest at a brothel.

Calculating in the last pot, Cotton figured how much

money he had wadded up in his pocket. He wished he could've emptied all his dough out on the floor, but the ache in his jaw reminded him of the moment. "Seventy, no seventy-five," he said, jumping up from his seat. "I bid seventy-five, right here, right now, and don't cut me for no five or ten buck bid. Make 'em beat me true."

"Mighty fine," the madam said, as pleased as finding lost money. "Who'll bid one hundred then?"

Cotton stepped next to the madam and the kitchen girl. "Anybody?" he said, scanning the room. Corley's face was sweating enough for a whole infantry platoon primed to go over the top the trenches, and the roofing group was as quiet as corpses. Tommy shook his head, slumping over, despite the continued prodding from Cobb. Pulling out his twisted wad of cash, he handed over his winning bid.

The madam counted the bills. "You got yourself a peach to pluck."

"Oh, no, not me," Cotton said, lifting the kitchen girl's slender wrist. He felt the fragile jut of the bone and her soft skin, glazed like Murano glass, but he'd learned there were times when you couldn't bear the cost of chasing every hand you were dealt. Extending her knobby weightless arm, he led her over to Corley. "Superintendent Brewer is the only one in this room man enough for this task."

"By God." Corley snatched her arm and tugged the kitchen girl toward the stairs.

Cotton faced jug-ears, his dense pal, and the rube, holding up his remaining cash. "I still got a few bucks if you gentlemen would care for another spin at the poker table. You too, Mr. Tommy, being as you got a little extra dough." For the first time all evening, the ache drained from his jaw.

.

Chapter 18

In the dim stairwell, Molly traced the vines that twisted through the carpet. She was glad the winner, the keen fellow in the jazzy suit, had handed her over to the old man; with each step up the stairs the poor geezer's exhales grew more strained. After a couple of grunts, he might croak in her bed.

Throwing his suit coat over the back of the chair, he plopped down on the side of the bed. "Secure that door."

Molly locked her bedroom door and went to return the key.

"Leave that to me," he said, holding out his hand. "And keep on the overhead light. Let's see what Captain Victory Medal paid for."

She dropped the skeleton key in his sweaty, plump palm.

"Take off my riding boots." He tucked the key in his pants pocket and raised up a leg.

The old man was brasher than the other auction winners, who required the seclusion of a darkened bedroom. Figuring he couldn't reach his feet, or see his johnson, Molly was satisfied hurrying the evening along. She grabbed his boot and gave it a tug, but it didn't budge.

"Put your backside in it, kitchen girl," he said, like he was ordering a county chain gang.

Molly yanked it harder, and the boot broke loose from his fleshy calf. After this sweaty geezer passed out, Molly was going to pick his wallet for more than a morsel. He had at least thirty extra, if not more.

"Make it easier on the other foot. Turn around, get that juicy rump in your work."

Straddling his stumpy leg, Molly turned her back to him and gripped his heel with both hands. She could her hear him fiddle with his belt, preparing to stroke himself. The other fellows usually called for a nudge before unbuckling their britches. It'd be a blessing if he passed out before he got his pants down, but Molly hoped he kept his wallet in his suit coat. She didn't want to roll his snoring sweaty ass over.

"I heard tell of you," he said between clenched teeth. "Strutting around to that jungle music."

Smiling at the thought of the growling singer and her becoming celebrities, Molly tugged on the boot and worked to remember if she'd ever seen the geezer before.

"Let me help me you out a bit." He planted his foot on her rear end and kicked her forward, freeing his boot and knocking her to the floor. Before she could get back up, he threw himself on top of her, pressing his girth onto her. He tore off her petticoat and jammed his fingers past the thick flesh of her cooch. "Being that you done sold off your slit before, ain't you more like a parlor girl than kitchen help?"

Fighting to wiggle out from under his suffocating belly, Molly gasped for breath, resisting the clawing of his chubby fingers.

"No hollering, the path to Mr. Zach's new road runs right between your legs, or there's about." He forced all his weight on her, his slimy whiskers scraping her back. "Your mouth looks warm, but you likely snap like a cooter in a creek."

"I'd gnaw off your teeny pecker and hock it out in the corner," she shouted, flinging her elbows into his ribcage. The failed blows drained the air from her lungs.

"What part of you is still virgin?" Mashing her head into the floor, he reared up and spit on her ass. "There ain't but one door left." The old man pressed his palm against her throat.

The pine floorboards ground at her chin, sandwiching her cheek and nose together. The bedroom turned on its end. A warm gob of saliva dripped down the crack of her butt cheeks. The overhead light sprouted from the ceiling, the bulb still blazing when she squeezed her eyes closed. She bit her tongue as he rammed his pecker in her bottom, bucking her hips against his pressure, each of his jabs ripping her supple flesh.

"Fight me, by God, that's good," he panted, leaning forward. "Your momma was a scrapper. She give you a dose of spunk." Thrusting over and over, he smacked his hips against her ass, grunting wildly, until he sputtered and twitched, tumbling onto the floor next to Molly.

Her arms and legs shook as she pushed herself up from the floor. In the naked sheen of the overhead light, Molly stood over the sprawled out old man and her mangled petticoat. She reached back and felt the blood and semen oozing from her bottom.

"Damn room spinning like a son-of-a-bitch. Help me up, girl." He extended his arm toward her.

The stabbing burn deafened his demands, and with her fingertips still sticky and moist, Molly picked up the fire poker.

"By God, I need a slab of ribs and a bed. Hey, now—"

The first blow cracked against his shoulder.

"Argh." He rolled over and scrambled toward the door, trying to stand up.

Molly bashed him across the back two or three times, driving him into the wall, but he careened off, charging her like a bull unleashed from a pen.

"You rotten cunny," he said, his droopy eyes now boiling white hot and wide. He caught Molly by the hair and slung her onto the bed. "I'll ring your whore neck."

Kicking at his chest, Molly battled to block his fist with the fire poker, but his punches battered the side of her head, ringing in her ears. She twisted her trunk to the side before he could dive across her belly, and she lunged back toward him, hammering the end of the handle into the old man's forehead. His head snapped back on impact. His eyes fluttered and then shut, and he keeled over onto the floor.

The fire poker clanked against the hearth as Molly tossed it down and bent over the geezer. His shriveled pecker poked out from his pants and an eggplant purple lump sprouted on his forehead. His eyes stayed closed. It was the keen bastard's fault. He was supposed to be up here in his jazzy suit, but he was undoubtedly a cream-puff who wouldn't enjoy a lady's mouth copping his doodle.

The old man snorted.

She could escape down the back stairs. In a rush, she scrambled to put on her best house dress and shoes. But what would she do? Steal a car? Molly frisked his suit and grabbed his wallet from his coat pocket, not bothering to look inside. Driving an automobile was much tougher than leading Stonewall and a wagon.

A seizure, that was the answer. The old geezer had busted a nut and fainted into the fireplace tools. Madam Mercier could protect her from the geezer. There was no way the madam would let them take her away when she still had sums on the owing side of the red ledger. Mr. Zach was a businessman. Whip Bannister owed Alma Mae some nameless obligation. Yet it was more likely that as soon as Molly ran downstairs, half-naked and hollering, Madam Mercier and Hinton would read her floozy face and know she was a no-account trollop the same as her mother. She couldn't be worth more than Hinton's road. Kneeling down next to the bed, she pulled out her twenty-dollar bill and the rest of her hidden cash from the mattress, tucking it in with the geezers. She rubbed her locket, still unsure of what she'd do once she was in the parking lot. She didn't possess a parlor girl's guile.

The geezer was no doubt blackout drunk. Claiming he honest-to-god passed out and rolled out of bed could be believed. Her father had done that countless times, waking up on the floor without a notion of last night. Molly retrieved the fire poker intending to flip him over and see if he stayed asleep. Like Skillet, maybe he wouldn't rouse until after sunrise, hankering for a drink of shine and a hot breakfast. But where would she be in the morning? Still at the lodge.

Still Hinton's whore. Still another of his earthly rewards for murdering her father. If the geezer had been a guest before, then the madam knew, Sally knew, and the parlor girls knew, that she'd been left alone with a buggering bully.

Extending his chubby fingers, the geezer reached for the hem of her dress.

Molly walloped his fatty ribcage three or four times with the charred shaft. The curved steel tip raking into the floorboards as he sunk back. The brass handle vibrated through her arms, into her shoulder blades, and down her back, resonating in the base of her spine.

Run.

Molly yanked on the door. It was locked. Bending over the panting old man, bloody spittle pooling at the corner of his mouth as he gulped for breath, she dug through his right pocket. It was empty. She moved to check the left one.

"By God," he moaned, snatching her thin wrist.

Standing up, she broke free from his grasp, and with the force of squashing a cockroach, she stomped on his exposed pecker.

Howling, the geezer balled up in pain.

Molly plucked the key from his pocket and scurried down the backstairs, untroubled as to what she'd do next.

Chapter 19

The pot was right. In the center of the poker table, Cotton figured there were four-hundred dollars. It was all the money he needed to settle his trickiest past-due accounts, stake him in Arch's Louisville game and spare him the burden of asking his boss for an advance, which his father would have to obliquely approve. If only Cobb and his pal would stop gabbing like two ladies on wash day, the drunk rube would finally fold and he could call.

"Goddamn, fella, if you'd play the right cards it'll help the whole damn table," Cobb said to the rube. "Hey, Tommy, he's like old Third-out Gilley, the rally killer."

"Played with us a season or two on the Tourists." Tommy hardly glanced up from his cards.

"Tried every slump-busting trick there was, holy water, rabbit's feet. Guaranteed to leave the bases loaded."

"That's him," Tommy said, agreeing with his legendary pal.

The rube closed his left eye and then his right eye switching back and forth.

Cotton recognized the flummoxed face of a drunk before their head hit the table. If the bruiser had been a loyal hand, he'd have gotten his boss man away before he passed out; most any lie would do, but Cotton had a full boat— a pair of aces and three queens.

"Anything work?" the fawning rube slurred like an oddly drunken whippersnapper asking his hero for a batting tip.

"You got any darkies around?" Cobb asked, grinning sideways at Tommy.

"What?"

"Colored gals?"

"Of course, this is Scots Station." The rube blinked like fireworks and alarms were sounding in his head.

"Screwing a darkie is a guaranteed slump-buster." Cobb leaned closer to the rube. "But Third-out would never give one a go. Ain't that so, Tommy?"

"Never would give one a go."

Wavering but still upright in his chair, the rube hollered over the giggling ballplayers, "Fetch one of Isaiah's pickaninnies."

The bruiser gave his boss man a cockeyed stare, glanced over at the madam dozing on a chaise lounge, and folded his arms across his chest, stepping further into the dark corner.

"Bannister? Don't be going soft again. You're simple, but you ain't deaf."

"Pardon the interruption, but were you considering if you'd be interested in raising or calling?" Cotton asked the rube, with the diplomacy of a first-class concierge.

With a sweeping pivot, the rube pointed a finger in Cotton's face. "How'd you get so damn lucky?" he said, as riled up as a billy goat.

The ache seared through Cotton's face, torquing his cheek muscles and grinding his jaw-bones together. "Trying to keep the game moving is all."

"Moving money from my pockets to yours. What else you got in your pockets?"

"No offense intended." Cotton held up both his hands.

"Here's what I got in my pocket," the rube said, exchanging a silver-plated Colt .45 for the crooked finger he'd pointed at Cotton. "Now let's see what you got in yours."

A dazed Cobb and Tommy eased their chairs away from the table.

"Hey, fella," Cobb said, "if you're fixing to shoot that hyena-grinning bastard, would you mind waiting until me and my friend stepped out for some air."

The bruiser moved out of the shadows.

Huns, Russians, Turks, Micks and Spics had all pointed weapons at Cotton, but it wasn't shiny loaded guns that tightened his gut. It was the fool with his finger on the trigger. He didn't wish to make his mother grieve over another lost son, or prove his father right by bleeding to death in a cathouse. A traveling peddler, gambler, or whoremonger, disappearing in a backwoods swamp at the order of a cow-pie county boss man wasn't farfetched. However, that was all the money Cotton had left in the damn world on the table.

"Mr. Jack, sir, I apologize for the trouble," Cotton said, forcing himself to nudge closer to the spread of rumpled bills covering the center of the table. "If you just let me get the pot—I got a full boat . . . trip' queens—I'll mosey—"

"Mr. Zach Hinton says, I got other means to check your pockets." The rube's eyes swelled wide.

"I got a chunk in that pot," Cobb said as he unbuttoned his collar. "Don't think you're scooping my dough up."

"You can't top a full boat, so that makes it my money."

"That ain't the point."

"It most certainly is the point. High hand wins."

"Nope, not in this situation."

"Nope? You know, he's got more than one bullet in that pistol. Corley might not be the only fella plucking a peach this evening." Cotton turned toward Cobb, providing the rube a narrower target. "Lucky you could hit a tad 'cause you don't know nothing about cards or fielding."

"I'll show you what I know about whipping a jackass," Cobb said, springing up from his chair.

"Zach, put that foolish pistol away," the madam said, now sitting on the edge of the chaise lounge. She stood up and walked toward the poker table. "You don't wanna be famous for murdering the greatest ballplayer on earth."

Glancing around the crowded room, the rube struggled to sort out the question and the answer. He lowered the angle of his Colt a degree or two and tossed his cards into the pot.

"Fly-ball dropping son-of-a-bitch has gotta die sometime."
Cotton stiffened his shoulders, squaring off across from Cobb,
like an umpire who'd had his fill of uppity bellyaching. Every
baseball fan in America knew the tales about his sharpened
spikes and him beating up a Negro groundskeeper, but
Cotton didn't necessarily believe the wildest rumor about him
attacking a crippled heckler.

"I'll throttle your sassy mouth."

"Maybe after you satisfy your fighting itch," the madam
said to Cobb as if they were the only two people in the room.
"You'll be ready to tackle the fucking one."

"I'll split my winnings with you, 50/50," Cotton said,
gathering up the pot. "That way you can tend to your other
business."

The legendary ballplayer eyed the madam as Cotton
separated the bills into two stacks. Her breasts peeked out
from the top of her beaded black dress.

"This is my share." Cotton crammed a stack into his suit
coat pocket. "And here's yours." He head-butted Cobb in the
bridge of the nose and rammed his knee into his groin. The
ballplayer reeled back, blood spewing between his fingers.
Dazed from the strike to his own head, Cotton snatched up
the other stack of money.

The rube raised the pistol over his head, pulled the trigger,
and rained plaster dust down on the poker table.

Cotton flipped over the tabletop, sending the rube
toppling to the floor. Dashing out the front door, he bounded
off the side of the porch, nearly twisting his ankle, and ran to
his roadster, not intending to stop until he got three or four
counties away, maybe even a state or two.

Chapter 20

In the parking area around the manor house, a three-quarter moon peeked out from the top of the magnolias, and the night air was warm without the draining humidity of summer, allowing Molly to dream she was taking a midnight jaunt to check the mail. But she knew the pleasant spring night lied. The automobiles were lined up in dark, uneven rows, like scattered caskets. The taste of her stewing stomach flushed up her throat, tempting her to pray for the first time in weeks. But she doubted the Savior was a trickster in a gleaming white robe, tossing her in the fire to later instruct her on the means to escape the flames. A convertible at the farthest end of the lot beckoned her over. She had seen the gold two-door coupe before, in a dream, or a stupor, stationed outside the lodge on some other night.

Sitting in the driver's seat, Molly stowed the stolen wallet down her dress. She gripped the gear shift looming up from the floorboard like an abandoned guidepost. The maddening array of pedals and levers would require a wizard to operate. She rested her head on the steering wheel. The side of her face ached like Stonewall had kicked her in the head. Blocking the stubborn burn between her legs, she could tell her lip was swollen, and the harsh taste of her own blood filled her mouth. She released a reddish dribble of drool.

A blast came from the lodge.

Molly popped up in the leather driver's seat. There was a crash, and then the thumping of footsteps from the keen fellow in the jazzy suit running up to the car. "Make this confounded contraption go," she said, shoving the fire poker in his face.

"Get your load out." Panting, the keen fellow snatched open the car door.

"My load ain't going nowhere." She pushed the tip of the charred poker tight against his chin.

"Then don't get out," he said, smacking the steel tip away from his face. He forced his rear end into the driver's seat. Molly clumsily slid over, keeping her poker trained on him. The keen fellow mashed a button and pumped the pedals. Molly resisted asking which side of the poker room had been shooting. He might be her salvation, a guardian angel in a jazzy suit.

The engine started, and he nudged the gear shift forward. He smashed another floor pedal, and they were rolling through the pecan orchard.

At the end of the driveway, they turned left on the main road. The breeze whipped at Molly and her arms ached. She lowered the poker, brushed the hair from eyes, and squirmed in the seat to find relief from the smoldering pain that burned a line from her cooch to her bunghole. They were heading the opposite direction from the Lingos' former farm.

"You know the roads around here?" he shouted above the road noise and the wind.

"Not at all," Molly said.

"I think there's a shortcut up here in a bit." The keen fellow glanced in the rearview mirror.

Molly turned around and saw the road lamps trailing them in the distance like Alma Mae's menacing eyes after she'd sassed her mother back. She squeezed the poker's brass handle.

The fellow swerved onto a side road and accelerated. The car skidded to gain traction as the slippery dirt lane narrowed and the roadside ditches grew deeper. His left arm straightened and he threw his right arm across her chest. The two-seater careened sideways, slamming to a halt a few yards before a fallen tree.

With a glare, Molly slipped out from under the pressure of his arm on her breasts and peeked ahead. A thick long-leaf pine tree as tall as the lodge blocked the road.

"Bloody hell," he said, returning both hands back to the steering wheel. "You wanna drive or move the tree?"

"I can't drive," Molly said, pulling strands of hair from her mouth. "And I ain't got a dozen field hands, or a team of mules."

Leaning up, the keen fellow stuck his head over the windshield "Too bad you can't fuck—"

Molly lunged to punch him, but he defended against her strike and she caught his arm instead. "At least, I didn't take the wrong shortcut like some lousy cream-puff." Her hand stung from smacking the bone in his forearm.

"Lousy cream-puff?"

"You the shooter or the shot at?" Molly said, borrowing her mother's tone. "I wanna make sure I'm not running with no murderer."

"I'll have you know, I was a decorated Captain in the AEF, a Victory Medal winner."

"Sounds impressive, but I still don't know who I'm with or why you're running."

"Cotton Arnold," he said with a quick tip of his felt hat. "Former salesman at the Tri-State Tractor Company."

"Molly Lingo, former nobody."

"*Enchanté*, I'm sure. And I wasn't actually shot at. Your boss man got riled up over phony allegations and decided to fire a warning shot. So why are you running?"

"Who says I'm running?"

"Don't matter to me, but we have an ill-tempered brothel owner and his brute following us. Before I ditched them."

"Whip?"

"That's the simplest guess." The fellow stepped out of the car and leaned over the driver's side door, rubbing his jaw.

Molly slumped down in the passenger's seat. The woods sealed in around her, seemingly tranquil, but she didn't have to the hear coyotes howling to know they were hunting.

"Doubling back is the soundest bet." The fellow got back in the car. "Not sure I can maneuver a U-turn on this skinny logging road." He elbowed the gear shift, turned around, and began reversing the car back toward the highway.

The gears whirred underneath Molly. His right arm was stretched across the back of her seat. The nighttime woods flooded past in reverse. He bumped the shifter, the car's humming ceased, and they were floating backward down a river. He applied the brakes, and they coasted to a stop short of the main intersection.

"Hold still," he said and hopped out.

Molly followed him around to the rear luggage rack. "Where we headed?" she asked, wishing she didn't sound like a lost child.

"Sorta late for that question, but I'll get you to Georgia." The fellow released the leather straps and opened the trunk.

"Atlanta?" She'd listened in on the lodge guests from there bragging about streetcars and department stores. Watching his shadowy form dig deep into the large chest, she heard a metallic click.

"Sure, sure, right on Peachtree Street, or close enough," he said, latching the steamer trunk shut. "Load up, little sister. Let's go."

Headlights blazed on, exposing the runaway couple. Molly clutched her weapon across her chest. Zach Hinton staggered out from the sedan barricading the entrance to the main road. He was dressed in the same suit he'd worn on Thanksgiving night, except now his necktie was undone, dangling around his neck, and his ash gray suit coat was screwed up around his chest.

"Looks like I'll be inspecting your pockets after all." A shiny pistol teetered in Hinton's hand.

"I wasn't hiding any cards." The fellow pointed a revolver squarely at the approaching Hinton. "You kept dipping your hand for the whole table to see. We'll tuck our guns back in our britches, and I'll mosey on."

"Nah, nah, don't think so, nah," Hinton said, seesawing in the lit road. "Is that my virgin whore?" He aimed his pistol at Molly. "Why ain't you sporting with Brewer?"

"Shoot him, before he shoots us," Molly whispered, shielding her eyes from the bright lights. Whip must've been waiting beyond the glare. She was certain Hinton could spot the lump under her dress where she tucked the geezer's wallet. He could detect the scent of stolen money. She wished she'd used the chamber pot before she'd left the lodge.

The keen fellow steadied his grip on the metallic black revolver. "He can't cipher which blurry image to shoot first. There's no claiming self-defense before a local jury."

"You done absconded with my whore?" Floundering for anything to balance himself, Hinton's words wobbled like his stance. "You two in cahoots? I'll relish gutting you both from the backside to the brainstem."

"Lay that murdering bastard out now." By now, Madam Mercier had most likely discovered that Molly had cold-cocked one of her high-dollar guests. The geezer could be dead, and she'd pinched his wallet, the whole slice. The madam would make sure that Whip dragged her back to the lodge. Madam Mercier would see that her kitchen girl was cornholed by every pimply guest and hairy field hand that could muster a stiff prick and a buck before Sally tossed her smoldering corpse in the pit next to her father. Molly swung the fire poker in front of her, flailing in the air for the crush of Hinton's bones, not caring that he was ten or twelve paces beyond her range.

"Boss man, you're a man of commerce, a shrewd fella." Cotton glanced to the side at Molly and lowered his six-shooter. "What say you and I strike a bargain?"

"Like that one you struck with Cobb?" Hinton replied. "Griping like a spoiled schoolboy with a beefsteak across his nose. Snooty son-of-bitch deserved all he got."

"Yes sir, and I gave it to him."

"What you got in mind?" Hinton waggled his Colt .45.

"I figure you had a hundred in the pot. So I give your money back, and I get along down the road where I belong."

"A hundred?" Hinton laughed. "You lying-ass tractor salesman."

"Alright, then," Cotton said, shaking his head. "Let's say two, and you won't ever have to worry about seeing this tractor salesman's ass again."

"What about my virgin whore?"

"She goes with me." The keen fellow stepped closer to Hinton blocking the rube's view of Molly.

"You know she ain't got no bona fide virgin cooch? Long before Brewer come along, some strapping Wall Street Jew plucked her first."

"No matter."

"You must surely be in cahoots. Now her momma was a fun poke. But her daddy was as dumb as a dead coon . . . still, there's gotta be an additional consideration," Hinton said, holding his hand up in the air and ticking off three fingers. "She's good sporting stock. There are damages to my ceiling. And her pap ran away owing me a debt."

Molly pushed past the fellow and screamed at Hinton. "Ran away? I've been told what you done out at the pit."

"Loony bitch. Like her momma. Ain't that right, Whip?" Hinton retreated two or three steps, but kept his shiny pistol aimed at Molly. "Make it five-hundred dollars, no, no, seven-fifty, yep, seven-hundred-and-fifty dollars."

"Damn, you tossing in a top-flight hunting dog and a case of your moonshine to boot?" The keen fellow asked.

"Seven-fifty and you and your misfit parlor girl get a pass."

"This is the best I can offer, boss man," the fellow said, pulling the stacks of bills out of his suit coat. "Probably close to five-hundred dollars in here, but I'll get that loony bitch and me out your way. We got a deal?" He pushed the two tangled stacks at Hinton's gut.

"Close to five hundred? I'm going soft, but I figure it's a deal then." Hinton stuffed the bills into his pants pockets. "Now, Whip, knock that hyena-grinning bastard and my virgin whore to their knees," he said, turning back toward the car. "We gonna show Mr. Georgia Peach how we handle troublemakers in Scots Station."

With a deep grunt, Molly hurled the fire poker like a warrior launching a spear toward Whip. But arching over the brightness, the first crack of the horsewhip forced her back as it knocked the pistol from Hinton's hand. The second one pulled his legs out from under him setting him on his on his backside, his head bobbing about.

"Whip?" Molly yelled, snatching up the pistol next to the sprawled out Hinton.

The horsewhip entangled Hinton's left leg, and Whip cinched it tight, dragging him to the car, as he would have a back-talking tenant or a slothful picker. Hinton's shouts were lost in his clamor for air, and Whip grabbed him by his necktie, heaving him in the backseat.

Molly took four or five strides closer to the sedan.

Sliding into the driver's seat, Whip spun the blue-coffin sedan around.

"Bloody hell, he should've done that two hours ago." The keen fellow said, slipping the revolver in his waistband and picking up four or five loose bills spread out along Hinton's swerving path to his car. "What do you say, little sister?" He crouched on the roadster's rear bumper. "Atlanta or bust?"

Walking past him, Molly settled back into the two-seater with a Colt .45 on her lap and a secret bounty nestled in her brassiere.

Chapter 21

At sunrise, Cotton passed through West Point, crossing the swirling Chattahoochee River into Georgia. Molly slept next to him, occasionally waking herself with a snort. In a few hours, they'd be at Creekside. His mother certainly would be there, but his father should be staying at their townhouse, tending to his office fiefdom, and leaving the family farm until the weekend. Cotton couldn't have scrounged more than five or ten dollars off the road, which wouldn't get him near Louisville, much less a stake in Arch's game. The runaway kitchen girl—the virgin-whore—probably didn't have much more than her clothes and her gumption. Money wasn't a worry to his mother; it was more of a nuisance, especially smudged bills that had been in-and-out of other people's hand. Dorothy Arnold could have enough cash in her handbag to set up him for Louisville, or buy him a ten-thousand acre cattle ranch.

The delicate morning sky illuminated Molly's curled-up figure. She was sixteen or seventeen, and she looked more virginal in her baggy dress than she had in last night's wrinkled camisole. Her hands were cut and cracked, her fingers a scalded pink, the tip of her nails a varnished brown. Every traveling mate, whether sharing a cushioned seat or sodden sandbags, had a tale to share about how they arrived and where they were headed. From the looks of her puffy bottom lip and bruised cheekbone, her tale of woe and desperation involved some type of fisticuffs or an ornery dairy cow. Hinton had undoubtedly earned her scorn, but Cotton wondered if in some hick town her folks were praying for their stray daughter, or if she'd been erased. Her dress flapped in the spring air, the tangerine polka dots fluttering like gum drop zephyrs. Glimpsing her lingerie strap, silky thin, he allowed his mind to slither past the V-neckline and tarnished locket. When they stopped at Creekside, he needed her to stay in the LaSalle, any story he contrived would burden his mother. But before he headed out on his own, he'd take her out for dinner in Atlanta, one of those new diners on Ponce with the chrome and the glitzy buzzing lights.

Cotton stuck his arm out of the side of the roadster, signaling for a turn he never intended to make, challenging the rushing air that surged through his fingers. The morning horizon over the jagged hills was striped with bands of orange and purple, the same as the unnerving sunrises in the French countryside— waiting for the chaos, stoking his courage with cigarettes and cognac. He could still see the trembling soldiers scratching their chin straps in pale dread of the whistle sending them over the top, a showdown between nerves and duty.

A cracker in a Model T passed by, and Cotton caught the sheriff's logo on the side. In the rear view, he spotted the old Ford's brake light. The sheriff made a hard U-turn at the supply store, and Cotton checked his speedometer. The pasty cracker was most likely turning around to harass some unlucky blackie tramp. He put both hands on the steering wheel and accelerated; his LaSalle roadster could outrun the county's jalopy. If Hinton was conscious this early, he couldn't ring up the state police to report an assault during a crooked card game, or a runaway kitchen girl. He pushed the gas harder, running the LaSalle near the top end. The closer he was to Creekside, the less trouble there would be, unless his father was there.

When Cotton opened the servant's door to his parent's house and crept down the back hall, he hoped to hear the wireless blaring from the drawing room. His mother, half-deaf, never listened to her shows when her husband was home; the "trumpeting triviality" wore his patience. Instead, there was silence and Adah's cramped grimace as she looked up from polishing silver. Lucius Arnold was home.

A line from Shakespeare, his top grade at military college, passed through his mind: *"Once more unto the breach, dear friends."* Crossing the threshold into his parent's sprawling drawing room, he tried to recall if the quote was from *Richard III* or *Henry V.*

His sable-haired mother was hunched over in her armchair, working on her needlepoint in front of the fireplace. She was wearing a tailored maroon dress in case an unforeseen visitor from the church came calling or one of her husband's business associates arrived.

"Bonjour, mother, top-of-the-morning," Cotton said, greeting her with a prompt peck on the cheek. "Sorry to barge in without adequate announcement, but I'm late for an appointment in Atlanta. I need to wash up." On the end table next to her were the remnants of her morning tea and scones, a stack of magazines, and a crystal vase of freshly cut flowers. He examined the sitting area for signs of his father. The door to his study was shut as always. "I had a dreadful night, entirely too far deep in the Alabama backwoods. Don't your tulips look marvelous? The bulbs from the Philadelphia Garden show? I'd say your experiment went smashing."

The oak paneled door to his father's study slid open, and Lucius Arnold, his navy-blue three-piece suit bandbox pressed and his light blue bow-tie square, strode in like a judge entering the courtroom. He stood behind his chair.

"Morning, father, I wasn't expecting to see you here." Cotton said, running his fingers through his rumpled hair, knowing from his tired and wet eyes that it was obvious he'd been up all night. The reek of the poker room, the sour cigars and sugary whorehouse perfume, clung to his bedraggled suit. "Just the gentleman scholar I can ask about a Shakespeare quote that's been taxing my mind. You have a minute for some trivia or are you headed to the office?"

Stepping out from around his wingback chair, his father held a tri-folded sheet of paper. "You care to tell me about your night in the Alabama backwoods?"

"The usual tractor selling business."

"This telegram I received from Birmingham states to the contrary."

"How so?"

"James Wakeman claims you were involved in a scandal at the Sporting Lodge, over near Scots Station. He heard it from his associates in Montgomery."

"No, sir, maybe a mix-up over a couple of cards, nothing more."

Lucius Arnold aimed the golden yellow message at his son. "Cornelius, I've been on the phone, long distance, with Wakeman and his affiliates."

"I was all square when I left last night, out a little money and sleep, but tip-top shape." Cotton said, concentrating on the neatly swept fireplace, the crisscrossing hardwood logs and the kindling wood stuffed below the grate; all ready for the match. "Looking good for closing the deal."

"The State deal with Superintendent Brewer?"

"Yes, sir, we're all good."

Her needlepoint jiggling on her lap, Dorothy Arnold focused on her oldest son's portrait above the mantle.

"I couldn't disagree more." Lucius Arnold paced a tight loop in the family sitting area. "Evidently, Superintendent Brewer isn't doing so well. He's in the hospital, and some miscreant, a Zachary Hinton, is claiming you and a . . . young woman . . . stole seven-hundred-and-fifty dollars."

"What? Who stole seven-hundred-and-fifty dollars?" Cotton asked, suppressing a laugh.

"According to Wakeman's report, you and a member of the lodge's staff robbed Brewer of funds this Hinton paid for engineering fees, doubtlessly a bootleg remuneration."

"No, no, no, sir, that's not what happened, impossible," Cotton stammered, shuffling away from his father's path. "Totally impossible."

"I have no reason to doubt James. He claims they've alerted the police force in both states. And contacted Blount's men, who are far worse than the Pinkertons if they hit upon money."

"This doesn't jibe." The sofa in between his mother and father's chairs beckoned Cotton to stretch out for a nap. Five or ten minutes of shuteye was all he needed to sort this out and find his way again. The pasty cracker in the jalopy had turned around for him, or for her.

"Of course it does. It's leverage. It's about money, more than seven-hundred-and-fifty dollars. Brewer is a Montgomery man, but don't presume he and Hinton couldn't still manage a certain influence under the Gold Dome."

"The Gold Dome?"

"Harboring you anywhere in Georgia could be a problem."

"Harboring me?"

His mother's gaze now pivoted from her husband to her son as if one of her radio shows were doing a live performance in her drawing room.

"Blount's agents are unrelenting. Posing as law enforcement, you won't see them in the shadows, Cornelius. I've heard they even employee female agents," his father said. He stopped pacing. "Where's your accomplice? Concealed in the LaSalle somewhere?"

"What does it matter?"

"We have to turn the harlot in, immediately, *auribus teneo lupum.*" His father stood as stark as a hitching post in front of the fireplace. "And wolves bite."

"So this all about protecting you and your business associates," Cotton replied. A maniac hum now fortifying him, he resisted the tightness clenching his jawline.

"You take after your mother's folks, your uncle Allan, and

not every returning soldier was a Rough Rider."

"Look away. Look away. We mustn't hamper the pursuit of transforming Lewallen County into smokestacks and company shanties. Dixie can be as wretched as any other New England mill town—pilfer the land, foul the water, coerce the families. Is that your stand?"

"Spare me the dragons you create to slay. The mundanity of your steerage class bravado is inappropriate for the occasion. There's no course but to turn in this strumpet thief and check you into a sanitarium. Allow you to rest for a spell."

Cotton stepped beside his mother's gracile armchair.

"*Festina lente*, father," he said in a level voice like he was responding in Morning Prayer. In a couple of days, his father could contact Wakeman, or the Blounts, offer to reach a settlement, deliver an envelope of cash, to protect his investment firm, his partnerships, and his Gold Dome cronies. Cotton could spend a few weeks reading, smoking cigarettes, and playing cards with the orderlies, but the mushy lumps of food would still stick in his throat like wet sawdust and the endless blathering of overblown flakes would fester in his mind. Besides, Miss Molly had more than silk undies beneath her orange polka dot dress. "Your route could be best, but at least allow me to feel like I'm not hasty."

Dorothy Arnold placed her hand low on her son's shoulder. "I'll have Miss Adah check to be sure you have a laundered shirt and a fresh suit. You'll feel more yourself after you freshen up; it'll all be sunnier," she said, with the faith that competent grooming supplied all the answers.

Smiling down at his mother, Cotton's exhalation clung to his lungs, and he was convinced he'd never be back at Creekside.

Chapter 22

Molly woke up alone in the front seat. A budding pecan branch hovered over the roadster. The crick in her neck tightened. She rolled out of the car, clutching Hinton's pistol. The butterscotch roadster was parked on the edge of an orchard, not far from a road. At the other end of the grove, on an earthen mound, was a gray manor house rising above a creek; its copper roof was a faded wiregrass green. The granite block front formed a frozen checkerboard.

The urge to pee strained her bladder. Molly hid the shiny Colt .45 under the passenger seat, and then snuck behind a scabby looking tree, lowered her underdrawers, and squatted. She licked her cracked lips, tasting a trace of blood and dried spit. The sluggish burning simmered in her crotch; what she wouldn't give for a cool creek to soak her buns or a bottle of the madam's witch hazel to dab on her cooch. The geezer's wallet plopped to the ground between her legs, and she sprayed it with a warm stream before grabbing it up. The sudden move nearly tumbled her over, but she righted herself, and wiped the wallet off on a patch of dewy clovers. Opening it, she thumbed past her thirty-one dollars to a string of fifties.

Her forehead drew up as she counted.

Five, ten, fifteen.

Seven-hundred-and-fifty dollars.

Her body, stiff and twisted from sleeping in the car, started to unwind. She imagined Skillet whirling about in an Irish jig if he'd ever found such a fortune. Putting the cash back in her brassiere, she stuffed the geezer's worn wallet into a mole tunnel at the base of the pecan tree, and returned to the roadster.

The stinging trace of cow manure drifted in the breeze.

Off in the distant woods, a sawmill gnawed on raw timber and a diesel motor played its steady dirge.

Cotton was hustling back to the car in a starched shirt, his blond hair slicked tight.

"You wash up in the big house and leave me to squat behind a tree?" Molly asked, angling her body and her voice away from him.

"My apologies," Cotton said, tinged with the reproach of a little boy who'd been punished. "I did you a favor." Sinking into the driver's seat, he handed her a wax paper present. "Here, sorry, it's not a country ham biscuit."

Ripping the greasy wrapping, she tore off a bite of the pastry. "We near Atlanta?" she asked, working to keep a big piece of the raisin-filled bun in her mouth and still let her words out.

"Yeah, I'm mean, no, not really close, but yeah."

His meandering doubt pried open a memory in her mind. Molly had heard it while they drove, an evaporating dream, a shallow puddle in the summertime sun. She was a nurse, and Rose was there with her. Cotton confronted another man in a muddy olive uniform, each shaking and wanting to flee. The harder she pursued the fuzzy memory, the faster it dissolved.

"I can take you to the West Point line," he said. "You can catch an afternoon departure to Five Points."

A train whistle's far-off blare and the ringing of metal hammering metal joined the harsh discord of noises.

Molly had only ridden a train once for school. She couldn't picture herself lined up in the lobby, buying her ticket through the iron bars, as befuddled as Alice falling through the looking glass; the grim conductor questioning where she put her bag, or why a pistol was on her lap, shiny or not.

"It arrives not too long after dark." A scrapper's tone returned to Cotton's voice. He bounced out of the roadster and raised the cowling, latching onto a familiar drill.

A split hull dangled from the end of the pecan branch like a gaping mouth.

Molly could see herself stepping out onto the rail platform, the perfect target for every big-city scalawag she'd read about.

"You might've whacked Brewer harder than you realize, but there's no going back to bring him a bouquet of tulips," Cotton said, inspecting the engine.

If Scots Station had one Hinton, Atlanta could have an army of traitorous rascals.

He closed the engine cowling and clapped his hands together. "I'm not a cream-puff, and I can be a gentleman. I'm going north, leaving Atlanta to the Yankees. I think we should give Chattanooga, or Nashville, a look-see."

After a few days and a few more states away, she could better decide where to settle. "Any place with restrooms so I can wash up?"

"Sure, sure, they got a Texaco near Nasonville, washing up makes the world sunnier," he said, back in the driver's seat pumping and pulling the buttons, levers, and pedals. "If you want, I'll take you for a chicken chow mein dinner in Louisville."

"You'll stop and let me buy some things before we get there?"

"Of course, might need you to spot me a couple of bucks until my commission check catches up." Beaming like a blue-ribbon winner, Cotton engaged the gear shift. "Won't be a problem."

Molly checked to be certain the geezer's cash wasn't sticking out from her dress. Any fellow connected to a granite mansion and a bustling estate shouldn't be asking her for money, but for seven-hundred-and-fifty dollars, Hinton and his cornholing partner would rush to track her down, the bastards hunting her like a runaway slave who'd stolen their heirloom seeds. She finished the last of the odd biscuit. The keen fellow in the jazzy suit might be the most notorious scalawag in two states, but gambling on him felt right in her body. The knowing sensation didn't sprout from her gut. It grew from her forehead, right above her eyebrows. The same area where she sensed her father and Rose at the pit, and where the voices shot up in her head. It, or they—the Holy Ghost, or Satan's Legion—told Molly she could count on Cotton to be a fine traveling companion. A craving for a dose gnawed on her nerves. She should've snatched the madam's bag, but that would've added yet another member to the gang wanting her sent back to the lodge.

The roadster roared ahead.

Pecan shells cracked under the tires.

And her grin widened with each burst.

Chapter 23

Studying the roadmap blurred Cotton's vision, and the pain gripped his jaw. What did his father know about steerage-class bravado? He'd never seen the lower deck of an ocean liner unless it had been in a shipyard.

"You really need new wiper blades, mister," the service station attendant said, scrubbing the LaSalle's windshield.

"Can't spare it now, governor," Cotton said, knowing any higher amounts would stand out when his charge account was reconciled at Tri-State's headquarters. Within a week or two, his father would see to it that he was officially terminated from his employment, after his mother had calmed down. She'd stare at his brother's portrait, Luke lording over the drawing room, his death mask cast with an eternal luster of confidence. Safety was now a luxury.

"You know what they say about April showers. How about a quote on a new set of tires?"

"Just waiting for the lady." The service attendant was waiting on her, too. Cotton had seen the tilt of his head following Molly's curves into the store. He'd bet any takers a twenty the scrawny attendant would scurry around to open her door when she came back.

Studying his map again, Cotton calculated that he had a good four-hundred miles and five or six days to establish himself as a sound investment. Blount's agents would probably focus their efforts on Lewallen County and around Atlanta. He could follow U.S. Highway 27 up through the western part of Georgia, his old route when he was peddling cleaning supplies for his uncle. Any outsider savvy enough to discover his former trail of boarding houses and ramshackle hangouts would be recognized, and the longer they eluded Hinton and

Brewer the easier it would be to make a deal if they got caught. He wouldn't mention the boss man's bribe. Let her believe she held a secret treasure buried beneath her polka dots, no benefit in turning her too skittish. A runaway kitchen girl's motivations weren't any different than his father's, and Lucius Arnold never invested a Buffalo nickel in anything less than a sound investment. The gripping ache surged beyond his jaw, gouging into his cheekbone.

Chapter 24

At the foursquare tent revival last autumn, the guest preacher, Brother Coe—a burly Cajun with a smooth tenor voice—had closed each nightly service by singing a new hymn, "He's Got the Whole World in His Hands," and for four days traveling in Cotton's convertible, Molly learned what those lyrics meant. She'd left behind the black gumbo dirt of Scots Station, forgotten like last season's harvest, and watched the soil change to slick red clay with alabaster streaks. Outcrops of granite became tree-covered foothills, and then looping mountain roads with blue sky vistas stretching out over the journey ahead. Cotton told her stories of the Civil War battles at Chickamauga—the River of Death—and Lookout Mountain. He knew the name of each river they crossed and how it meandered its way to the Gulf of Mexico. Whenever they passed road construction, he told her the difference between a bulldozer and belly pan scraper, and how much commission you could earn by selling each one. They snickered at the silly names of towns, told dirty jokes, and wise-cracked about every gawking service station attendant. She saw her first high-rise hotel in Nashville, but they slept behind abandoned barns or thickets of overgrown brush. After four nights, her loins stung less and the gentlemen's whiskey went down smoother. They passed the bottle while Cotton's pointed out the figures hidden in the stars until she snored. She was unfettered, yearning to remember every naughty tale about a farmer's daughter who'd forgotten to wear her knickers and every celestial sign. From the formless void, God had created the earth and filled it with no-account trollops, murdering skinflint bastards, and pot-bellied old geezers, who all deserved what they received.

All she needed to prosper was wisdom not to be duped.

The thunderstorm didn't hit them until after sunset, well after they crossed the Cumberland River and made it to Horse Cave, Kentucky.

"God damn wipers," Cotton said, leaning over the steering wheel.

"I'd be drier if I'd jumped in a lake." Molly wrung out the hem of her dress onto the floor-board. The pinging rain had drenched them before they got the top up.

"We're gonna have to stop for the night."

"Wet to my knickers."

"I know a place a short hop away, a rooming house, mostly for salesmen."

"It'll give me a chance to try more of my new Woolworth's."

"The proprietors are Primitive Baptist."

"I was one of those once," she said, laughing and reaching between Cotton's legs for the bottle. "I was, I was, I was." She took a long swig, the whiskey blunting her cravings for a dose.

The roadster bumped across a set of railroad tracks, and glided through a right turn. Through the fogged windshield, Molly spotted lights, but the house was shielded by the evening storm.

Cotton turned into the circular driveway, parking as close to the front door as he could without crashing into the flowerbed.

Molly took another drink.

"The little fellow doesn't mind you having a hint of whiskey on your breath." He veered into the passenger seat, grazed her breasts with the back of his hand, and nabbed the bottle from her grasps. Cotton took two or three gulps.

"We got more than a hint." In the murky glow of the gas porch light, Molly saw the jut of his chin as he titled the bottle back, and she could taste his salty scent lingering on her palate.

"They charge enough to see past drunkards, but not

fornicators." He reached into his shirt, pulled a chain from around his neck, and unclasped it. He handed Molly a thin gold ring.

Molly rolled the slender band between her fingers. "Where'd you get this?"

"I may have won it in a card game, but the old fellow's battleax wife would call the law if she thought we were acting immorally."

"Does this mean you're getting us the honeymoon suite?"

"First you accuse me of being a cream-puff," he stuck the whiskey bottle in his inside coat pocket, "and now you're dying to consummate our counterfeit nuptials."

"You'd never be so blessed to knock my noggin against the headboard," she said, wiggling the ring over her knuckle. At the crown a flower blossom gracefully rose from the gold. The clinking of the storm against the roadster diminished, and the snug front seat was cozy. The whiskey and the delicate band uncoiled a warm tickle at the bottom of her belly.

"It's slacked up, let's make a break for it," he said, draping his suit coat over his head.

"Last one inside is a rotten egg." Molly flung open the passenger door and shrieked as she dashed for the front door.

Lying back on the pillow, Molly tightened the belt on her new bathrobe. The store clerk had called the color Copenhagen blue, and Cotton had joked about eating Danish pastries. After her warm bath alone, that itself a godsend, the satin was lush on her skin, finer than the madam's outdated camisole, and she traced the embroidered petals with her crinkled fingertips. She peeked through the opening in the bathroom door. Cotton was standing in front of the mirror in his light brown trousers, striped suspenders stretching across his bare shoulders. He was shaving for the first time since they'd been on the road, his head angling to the side, his wiry back bending forward, and his thick fingers leading each stroke of the razor across his face.

The floorboards creaked outside their door. The coy pause between footsteps meant it was the old woman who ran the boarding house. Cotton had attempted to charm her with his warm hug, talking of how bad the rain was but how he and his new bride had driven through the storm so they could be here in the morning for her silver-dollar pancakes. The creak edged closer to their bedroom door. Cotton came out of the bathroom, patting his face dry. Raising herself up on the pillow, Molly picked the whiskey bottle off the bed and took a long sip, leaving the bottom of her robe open above her knee.

"Watch yourself, Mata Hari, no need to be swinging off the canopy. The old gal really goes for her old-time religion," Cotton knelt with one leg up on the edge of the bed, "like you do."

Molly passed him the bottle; aware her bare breasts were poking out from behind the blue crease. "Did." She knew the innkeeper's wife, her face as bitter as shriveled fatback, didn't trust the story of their honeymoon at the Derby. She'd stood behind her shrunken husband with her knotted stare, as he handed the room key to Cotton, murmuring her instructions. She was a Believer who'd revel in uncovering Molly's sins.

Cotton took a short sip, corked the bottle, and tossed it down on the bed. "You ready to hear about the new-fangled religion? The Lord's latest revelation delivered directly to Captain Arnold."

"What's that?" she said, charting his torso. His earthiness was now masked by the peppery fragrance of hair tonic and after-shave.

"God created men and women to fuck and eat fruit," he said with the conviction of a spirit-filled evangelist making an altar call.

"My, my, captain, I ain't never read that in my version of the good book."

"You aren't reading it right." Cotton was all on fours crawling towards her.

"You hunting for a bowl of berries and cream?" Extending her legs out on the bed now seemed as liberating as riding in the butterscotch roadster.

"Maybe later." He peeled back the fold in her robe and reached to kiss her.

Her lips parted to meet his, and Molly kissed a man for the first time, not a farm boy on an October hayride or a soda distributor paying for the privilege, but her rescuer on a half-canopy bed coasting down a mountain road.

Cotton kissed a path down her neck, his tongue flicked at her nipple, and he moved his lips across her belly, nestling his mouth between her thighs.

Arching her back, Molly moaned, oblivious to the envious creaks. The dour old biddy could listen to every squeak and squeal for all she cared.

Deep in the night, Cotton's arm was draped over her waist, and he groaned and shifted, waking her up. Disoriented in the unfamiliar room, fragments of a nightmare wafted past her. A team of horses buried to their gaunt bellies in the muck. Withered trees stretched along a scorched ravine. A trembling soldier cried out. Cotton whimpered in his sleep, and Molly drew his arm closer. The touch of his leathery skin against her ribs buried the dying warriors' desperate pleas for Captain Arnold.

Find out how sex and sexuality reveal Molly's development by subscribing to Southern Fried Karma's YouTube channel, Fugitive Views.

Chapter 25

Light invaded the borders of the blinds. The piquant aroma of their sex quelled the smell of bleach and lye soap. Cotton took a drag of his cigarette, flicked the ash onto the floor, and hunched over in the chair. His tailbone was planted like a pike in the wooly cushion of the lounge chair. He needed a teaspoon of whiskey to settle him. He'd been up in the Argonne with Harrison. A meager shot of brown liquor would cure the memory, but the bottle was lost in the wild knot of sheets, and judging from the hammering in his skull it was most likely empty.

Molly stirred, rolling away from the center of the bed.

There were enough new Texaco stations along the road to allow Cotton to charge his petrol to the company, but he'd almost blown the last of his cash to pay for the room. His stake for Arch's game was down to a couple of bucks. If he'd been traveling alone, he could've slept in the LaSalle or kept driving through the storm. This whole mess with Blount's people and Hinton pursuing him was his father's fault. The same as every wrong turn in his life. His unremitting scrutiny made Cotton reckless; it was an account he never could settle. Now, he only had a hundred miles and six or eight hours left to convince a fugitive whore to trust him with her money. The prudent solution would be to abandon her, leave her and her stolen money with the Grahams, and return home to live in the back cabin at Creekside. She could work in the kitchen until another traveling peddler came along. She could hustle. She'd survive.

Cotton monitored her gentle breathing, ensuring that she was still asleep. Her enticing contour was outlined in the dawn, a slumbering statue of Aphrodite. She was nearly half his age, and he could never present her to his parents, but his cock sprang alive. Perhaps Lucius's counsel to "put his hand to the plow" was a more pragmatic remedy; it was his father's perennial advice that he'd been giving since they packed a young Cornelius off to join Luke at Georgia Military College. He snuck back into bed and pressed himself against her ass, rocking back and forth. She welcomed him with a faint jiggle of her hips from side to side. With a smooth thrust, he recast her soft exhales into panting gasps.

Chapter 26

The fossilized old gal banged the pancakes down on the table, and the pewter serving platter put out a muffled clank, like a bell with a busted clapper.

Molly flinched.

"Not sure you followed me yesterday evening in all that scuttling and rushing," Ma Graham, the innkeeper's wife, said, standing at the end of the dining table with her chest thrust out. "Rock of Ages" leaked in from the kitchen. "But we serve breakfast at eight o'clock, spot on the mark. Most of our guests are enterprising family men who can't afford to lollygag away the heart of the day."

"Yes, ma'am," Molly said, regretting having to leave her half-canopy shelter. The dining room was suffocating in the morning light.

"The Lord only gives us a set number. Foolish to fritter them away."

"Yes, ma'am."

"I appreciate you accommodating us," Cotton said, stabbing at the stack of silver-dollar pancakes with his fork.

"Your own blame for missing the last of the pecan syrup and the table butter, Captain Arnold."

"You remember how it is when love speaks." He winked at Molly and poked her with his elbow.

Shifting her rear end to the edge of her dining chair, Molly mustered a grin for her accomplice, but the sturdy hardwood chair was as awkward as a church pew.

"The sluggard is wiser in his own eyes than he is in the Lord's, or mine," Ma Graham said, staring down at the couple with folded arms. "Mrs. Arnold, you care for some breakfast?"

Molly pulled at the sleeve of her new dress; it was snugger

this morning than it had been in the store and the yellow was too bright for breakfast. In the dim light of the fitting room, it had reminded her of dandelions, but in the clean boardinghouse morning it looked more like the watery yolk of a greasy fried egg. Her stomach churned. The freeing glow of the gentleman's whiskey was gone with last night's stars, leaving only its remnants—a parched mouth, an aching temple, and a twirling heat in her gut. She needed a dose of the madam's elixir, only a flood of raw pleasure could mend her ailing body and mind.

"Mrs. Arnold, are you going try a bite of the silver-dollar pancakes you nearly drowned for?" Ma Graham said, shifting her stance wider.

"Oh yes, ma'am," Molly said, sliding a couple of pancakes on her small plate, unable to deflect the old lady's burrowing frown. The tops of the pancakes were burned a darkish brown. Before they could come down for breakfast this morning, she'd had to hunt for her locket and her ring, and the penalty for upsetting the old biddy's routine was a platter of pancakes that resembled sun-bleached cow pies more than silver dollars. She spun the wedding band around her finger until the petite flower blossom was on top.

"I fiddled with my ring when my husband and I were fresh married." The innkeeper's wife displayed her arthritic left hand. "I met Mr. Graham at a revival meeting. He was rigging the tent, collecting the alms, and singing in the quartet." A skinny band of dull silver was fettered to her gnarled ring finger like a yoke around a claw. "I see your husband doesn't wear a wedding ring."

Molly cut her stack of charred pancakes in half and crammed her mouth full. She nudged Cotton's foot.

"Perils of the tractor-selling business," the captain said. "You don't wanna snag your finger."

"We had another guest here earlier in the week headed to Louisville. Stayed a night or two ago."

"Is that so?" Cotton replied not looking up from his food.

"Claims he was one those new G-men. I didn't ask for no badge," Ma Graham said, stepping across the dining room on the opposite side of the table. "He says when they hold that Derby that town is like a mongrel mutt in season, a teeming cauldron of Sodomites and white slavers."

"By golly, what's a G-man look like exactly?" Cotton asked, stroking the scant stubble on his cheek. His eyes now tracked the innkeeper as she moved nearer.

"Can't say about all of them, but this one was an odd-looking dainty type, sorta broad-beamed. Told Mr. Graham he was from Chattanooga, but his new model Ford had an Alabama tag," Ma said, grabbing the top rail of the chair across from Molly. "You ask me, the whole white slaving business ain't nothing but older scoundrels fooling homely dimwitted girls."

Molly swallowed another bite, but the pancakes settled like rebellious tailings in her belly.

"Everett, is that phone line back up?" Ma Graham yelled, daring the words not to make it past the kitchen door. "That storm you two brought with you took out my phone line."

The fluttering radio station grew louder, the gospel choir droning on for eternity. Molly pulverized the last dry crumbs of her pancakes between her clenched teeth. Laying her fork and knife across her plate, the thought of ramming the soiled cutlery down Ma's throat tumbled around in Molly's mind. Choke her on homely and dimwitted. This prig wouldn't care to send her back to Scots Station to face punishment. The foul old biddy couldn't know an iota of the torment that drove a woman to cut and run.

"You have you a big fancy church wedding?" the innkeeper's wife asked, leaning in.

"Oh no, ma'am. We didn't get married in a church, or nothing. My ma and pa are gone, practically vanished," Molly said, with a skittish lilt the madam never added to her auction preamble.

Ma Graham's nose crumpled together like a dried-out fig.

"Our family farm got swept away in the Tri-State tornadoes two springs ago." Unbuttoning her sleeves, Molly decided she'd wear the blue dress for their celebration dinner tonight. Cotton had promised that the deep blue satin would shimmer against the fine white table clothes at the Brown Hotel. "I'm the only one that made it to the shelter in time. My pap went back for my ma and little brother, but they were all carried away when the storm lifted up the house, smashed it to smithereens, and nearly scattered them to Georgia." In a city that was as notorious and as wicked as Louisville appeared, there had to be a friendly doctor offering ladies a potion to cure their ills. "I was studying nursing at the church college near Atlanta when I met Captain Arnold. I was kitchen help, part-time, at a lodge near Five Points, or I was." Molly held her ring up and wiggled her fingers. "Charmed me like King David."

"Uriah the Hittite could testify about David's intentions." Ma Graham cleared a load of phlegm up from her throat.

"I ain't so sure about all this King David jazz, but these pancakes are so delicious they don't need syrup or butter. I might need me a morning nap," Cotton said, tilting back in his chair. He stretched his arms towards the ceiling and yawned. He gave Molly another nudge and a wink.

The innkeeper's wife pulled her apron to her mouth and spat into it.

Molly shoved her dirty dishes across the table. "Too bad you can't afford a kitchen girl yourself, Ma," she said, grasping Cotton's thigh. "Captain Arnold, there's no time for any morning shenanigans. We need to skedaddle if we're gonna have a honeymoon feast in Louisville fit for a king and his new queen."

Chapter 27

The oak paneled walls at the English Grill in the Brown Hotel were lined with spotlighted portraits of horses, golden-framed paintings carrying brass name tags.

"How come they got no people hanging up?" Molly said, hiding her shoes under the tablecloth. Cotton was right; her deep blue dress flashed like a wild violet in a field of table linens, but her torn sandals betrayed her as an Alabama hick. Tomorrow, she'd buy a brand-new pair, or two, at one of the tall stores lining the street in front of the hotel. She slipped off her dowdy black sandals and tucked her bare feet further under the milky white tablecloth, which hung as long as any lady's gown she'd ever seen.

Cotton folded his newspaper up and placed it on the table. "Because nobody remembers the hay burners."

The waiter approached their table. "Good evening, Captain Arnold, such a pleasure to see you again," he said, handing them each a rouge red leather-bound menu.

"Good to be seen, Clifford, my friend," Cotton said. "Good to be seen."

Unfurling her napkin, the svelte waiter assisted Molly in placing the stiff linen cloth into her lap. She'd never see a grown man in a black tie, suede vest, and apron, but she recognized the same fake tone the parlor girls used. She imagined that out in the alley behind the hotel he pitched pennies and joked about clumsy restaurant guests.

"Can we offer you and the lady a refreshment before dinner?"

"John Barleycorn still in town?" Cotton picked up his own napkin.

"As long as you pay an adequate contribution to Mr.

Miller." The waiter gestured toward a gentleman dining alone in the opposite corner.

"I'll have a brown plaid with ice and a splash of seltzer water."

"And for the lady?"

"And the lady will have the mint julep," Cotton said, winking at Molly. "How's that sound?"

"Perfect," Molly said, not fully following the mysterious code that Cotton had begun speaking when they arrived in Louisville, but winking back regardless.

"Splendid, Captain Arnold," the waiter said, rearranging the salt and pepper shakers. "I'll bring the aperitifs straight away." The slinky waiter straightened the butter knives on the bread plates and swiped at the edge of the table with his bread crumber. Rotating his cufflinks, he inched a half-step closer to the captain. "The house cop always dips his beak first."

"Sure, sure, cash is king," Cotton said, reaching into his coat pocket and handing the waiter a buck.

"Excellent. Give me a moment, and I'll be back to go over the menu," the waiter said, spinning on his heels and walking away.

After watching him retreat, Molly turned to examine the shellacked canvas above their table, a chestnut thoroughbred posed in front of a black rail fence bordering a flowing green meadow. The engraving below it read, *Joe Cotton 1885.* "Look at that, you and this one almost got the same name."

"Yeah, the funny thing about that one," Cotton said, glancing up from the menu. "He broke his leg soon after that. I think it was at Mystic. They put him down right at the track." He pointed his index finger at his temple like a pistol and raised his eyebrows with a smirk.

"So he called you Captain Arnold, and other folks call you Cotton, but I'm sure you weren't born with either one of those names."

"Oh, no."

"So what's your real name?"

"Not telling."

"Our bogus marriage will never last if you keep secrets," Molly said, considering the consequence if a suspicious lawman ever asked her the same question.

"Not in a million lifetimes."

"It's gonna be a short honeymoon at this rate," Molly giggled.

"Cornelius, but when I was born my older brother said I was as soft and pale as a ball of cotton," he said, bending his evening newspaper into a neat square. "I'd toast all of you—my new queen, my family, dearly departed and otherwise—if I had my cocktail." Cotton raised his hand in a mock congratulations. "But where are your people?"

"Vanished."

"No, truly, where are they?"

"That's it," Molly said, picking up the silver butter knife from the bread plate. "Temptation snatched up my father and cast him across the river. Got him buried in a burned pit." She ran her thumb back and forth along the curved edge, catching her reflection in the polished blade. "And my momma's free will lifted her up and scattered her away."

"We'll toast to them, too."

"My pap would join you in a toast, or twenty. But ain't no toasting to Alma Mae Lingo." Setting the knife back on her butter plate, Molly switched it around from side-to-side until she had it in the exact position as the waiter did. She studied the various shaped spoons and forks spread out in a sterling plot of ground in front of her. The waiter had to be crafty if he could remember the convoluted layout for all these silver pieces and talk with a guest about bootleg booze at the same time. After her shopping mission, she'd wander around the block and see if she could find the backside of the hotel, where the staff lounged between shifts. The waiter could be as odd as an owl, but he'd point her in the direction of a dose doctor for a two-bit handy.

Welcome is every organ and attribute.

"So we really staying for the Derby?" Her face drifted to the center of the table.

"Sure. It'll blow your knickers all the way off."

"I hope so."

"Arch, you'll meet him, he's a good egg, he's got all the players—the blokes with the real scratch—landing to roost here at the Brown." Cotton leaned in joining Molly. "I got a business proposition for you."

"Say it ain't so." Molly said, a craving for the sting of the needle and the invading rush of heat in her veins.

"Listen, I know you're no dumb Dora, so I'll shoot you on the level," he said, cupping his hand over hers. "You stake me three or four hundred bucks for Arch's poker game, and we'll divvy up the winnings, fifty-fifty."

"What makes you believe I got three or four hundred bucks?" Her lips compressed into a single line of gloomy flesh.

"Play it how you want but that bell has been rung." Cotton tightened his grip on her hand. "There's a heap of authorities, lawful and not so lawful, hunting us both, including Ma Graham's bogus G-man. Hell, for seven-hundred-and-fifty dollars that greasy-eyed Jack Miller can't be trusted." He tipped his head toward the same man the waiter had earlier. "I know for a fact he buried union meddlers at the mines around Birmingham."

From her vantage, all Molly could see of the man sitting alone in the corner was his stock of coarse dark hair and his blubbery neck.

"Your keenest escape route heads you so far from here, you won't be able to remember the bowed floors of that slanted roadside shack you called home," he said, tugging her arm closer. "This is the time and the town to make a bankroll and bust out for Shangri La, or California, and not risk returning to the stench of Alabama outhouses in August, or worse."

"You must have been the star in all of the school shows."

Molly slipped her hand out from his and picked up her menu.

"Is this easy for you?" Cotton asked.

"Easy? I'm lost merely ordering dinner—what'd you call it?"

"Don't sweat it. Trust me to order for you."

Molly scanned the first two pages of the menu, the cursive swirls steering her journey.

"The hot brown is the new front-runner. You like turkey?"

"Nah, too gamey," Molly said, curious what advice Alma Mae would give her now.

"The chicken a la king is swell, too."

Reading the poultry dishes' elaborate description, Molly realized they'd taken the same simple ingredients from the lodge's larder and baked it in a pastry. But it was no longer Lizzy's chicken pot pie—it was a new recipe. One that wouldn't be found in Madam Mercier's crumbling cookbook back in the lodge. Molly knew if the madam sauntered into the hotel grill, she could decipher the best way to procure the finest shoes, have the waiter fetch her a dose, and game Cotton's scheme before dinner was over. But she was likewise certain that if the madam were here now, she'd be apt to put a derringer ball in Molly's forehead first and snatch Gabe's twenty-dollar bill from her corpse's garter.

The waiter returned with their drinks. "Have we decided anything yet, Captain Arnold?"

"You want me to order for us?" he said, smiling across their corner table.

"Whatever you say, Cornelius. I'm sure it'll come out fine, perfect." She sipped her sickly sweet refreshment.

Cotton took a swig from his mug.

Tickling her bare feet on the silky carpet below the table, Molly admired the poised rise of his cheeks amidst the collage of past champions.

A thickset woman approached the man in the corner and sat down across from him.

Cotton turned to examine the couple. "Who's Miller's gal pal?"

The petal-pink yoke around the woman's black gown made it appear like her head was set on top of a carnation.

"Miss Ellis? Been here a night, or two, says she's from Chattanooga," the waiter said, standing at nonchalant attention. "But she's never heard of The Reed House."

"Poor woman's frock reminds me of a perfumed sow at the county fair. But anywho, here's to busting out," Cotton said, hoisting his short glass mug. "Cheers."

Molly clinked glasses with a thirsty grin and, as Cotton turned to inspect the curious couple further, gave the waiter a wink.

Chapter 28

A layer removed from the city, Cotton lounged on a sofa in the lobby, isolated from the boulevard's glut of delivery wagons and the trace smell of barnyard shit they supplied. He scouted the simmering kettle of fashionable hotel guests smiling as they entered and exited the front door. He tried to recount how he had made it to the room last night. At their celebration dinner, he and Molly worked out a tacit agreement before they'd had too many cocktails and spent the rest of the meal babbling and planning picnics and globetrotting adventures in deluxe Pullman cars and ocean liner staterooms. They'd avoided a run-in with Miller, but Samuel, the bald night shift elevator operator, had helped him usher Molly down the hall. There was a sketchy memory of him coaxing his faux bride to flaunt herself in front of the mirror before they gave out. Earlier that morning, after she'd left to go shopping, he'd checked his billfold and found only a couple bucks left, which explained the pint of Indiana corn liquor in his suit coat pocket, as well as Samuel's assistance. His room-charge privileges would have to carry him until they could finalize their deal. Yet, consummating the final terms of their bargain with her would be taxing. He imagined himself as a store clerk haggling with the farmer's wife over the price for her eggs.

The lobby door swung open.

The city's rattling jackhammers overran the Brown's serenity, followed by a flourish of Arch's laughter as he recognized his fellow soldier.

"Would you look at what the B&O hauled in?" Rising from oval sofa, Cotton stuck out his hand.

"Cap, I wasn't sure you'd make it." Arch straightened his travel-creased vest and coat.

The two mates smacked each other on the back and shook hands like they were sawing logs, a familiar hello that had replaced a formal salute long ago.

"How was your journey?" Cotton asked.

"Troop train or private passenger car, there's nary a difference." Arch replied. "You take the express up from Nashville? How was the Hermitage?"

"Nah, I drove my automobile—it was a breezer, style and speed," Cotton said, mimicking the slick sales brochure from the dealer showroom. "I picked up a traveling comrade along the route, a pretty sensible gal, but down on her luck for a spell."

"Does she help with product demonstrations? Show the prospects the implements?" Arch swatted his old friend on the back one more time.

"Nothing like that," Cotton said with a wobbly trace of doubt. Arch would never picture Molly as more than a hustler laid out on a brass bed if he'd told him that he saved her from a whorehouse, and now wasn't the time to disclose that she was his potential banker. That he was her suitor. "I've about had a belly full of hornswoggling politicians, peckerwood tycoons, and hayseed engineers."

"We syndicated a manufacturing outfit, north of Chicago. They're searching for a man to peddle their new steam shovels—damn contraptions are iron beasts."

"I'm counting on your game launching me down the lazy river." Stretching his hand up toward the ceiling, a buoyant beat returned to Cotton's voice.

"Big Billy and Irish Monk are coming in for a game tonight. You got your stake covered?"

"Of course, I came prepared to do battle."

"They aren't like that Kraut tart at the end of that Anatolia fracas. The one at that musky pub near the Golden Horn. What did she say?"

"You're a little bit short, darling," Cotton added a

Continental nasal to his female impersonation. The two men shared a breezy gratified laugh as if they'd stepped from a waterside bagnio into the Brown Hotel lobby.

"So am I allowed to meet your comrade in arms and legs, or is she reserve stock?"

"Of course, I figured we'd have an aperitif this evening, a couple of pops, before the game." Cotton hesitated on bragging on how well she could recover from a bender. There was no doubt that Arch would recognize her ring—it had been his talisman since before the war.

"Speaking of, I need to huddle with Mr. Miller."

"He's around. I saw him having dinner with an actual dame." Cotton considered offering his chum a nip from his bottle, but the sunny noontime lobby didn't provide the same cover as an ancient alleyway. If Arch had arranged a game for tonight, Molly would have to bankroll his seat at the table. Without him, she was a bumpkin traveling on her own who couldn't order dinner.

"You'll have to tell me more about all this later on." Pulling his silver hunter-case watch from his vest pocket, Arch sprung the lid open and checked the time. "See you at the bewitching hour."

"See you then," Cotton said, taking out his own watch as Arch walked away to the reception desk. They'd never agreed on a time for Molly's return. He was largely comatose when she'd pranced out of bed, humming a homey gospel song. Memories of Lucius Arnold's lectures on frittered opportunity replayed in his mind, extinct Greek philosophers and Roman historians castigating him before he was born. Hard cash was the globetrotter's fuel. Cashing a bad check at the front desk wasn't an option. He couldn't risk drawing too much of Miller's attention, or any bogus G-man trailing him; hanging paper would land him a stint on the chain gang. Cotton searched for the lobby boy. Molly couldn't have ventured too far beyond the lobby. The young lobby boy could point him to the nearest store. A curvy single bumpkin girl wouldn't be difficult to spy. The savvy dippers and grifters probably had a spotter on the sidewalk outside the Brown, but she couldn't've been hit by a crafty cutpurse or taken-in by a slick-haired conman between the hotel front door and the closest department store. Cotton glanced over at the reception desk. Arch had the young lobby boy, bellhop, and doorman all occupied receiving instructions. Retrieving the bottle from his suit coat pocket, a good four fingers of clear sweet corn whiskey remaining, Cotton took two deep swigs. If he were truly ready to best the cardsharps, he'd locate Molly before he finished the pint bottle.

Chapter 29

The doorman held the tall glass door open for Molly and tipped his brown cap as she crossed over the lobby threshold into the street in front of the hotel. His sunny smile and long arm span reminded her of one of Lizzy's sons. But before she could recall which of them he most favored, the crowd—a tight bundle of spotty faces and accents—sucked Molly along in their current.

In the center of the cobblestone street, a clump of men jostled around a noisy puffing gadget that seemed to be better suited for demolishing rather than constructing. The hubbub swallowed the overcrowded street, filled with a hundred more merchants and offices than in Scots Station. Clattered calls of unseen mechanical creatures echoed in the sliver of blue sky above the hemmed in row of buildings. Molly followed the hurried crowd to the rhythmic clomping of horse hooves on the hard, round pavers. Down at the river landing, the crowd eased but the smoldering piles of road apples, heftier and ranker than near the hotel, reminded her of home.

Opposite the docks, a strip of stubby wooden buildings leaned in a wobbly group like rowdy lodge guests. Molly guessed they were saloons. A warm plate of fried eggs with pepper sauce and two or three cups of chicory coffee would heal her hangover. She'd left Cotton's ring and all but few dollars tucked in the nightstand bible, certain that the motley chambermaid wouldn't dare to steal Gabe's twenty from between the pages of Luke's gospel. As long as she had her timeworn bill she could always find her own path, whether the gate through was wide or narrow only mattered to, not her.

Dodging the draft horses and their loaded down wagons, Molly lifted up the hem of her dress and eased across the muddy unpaved street. A sour beer in a rusty pail with lurking white slavers would serve as the best route to find her a dose, but it was a risky breakfast. Once she bought her shoes, she'd track down the waiter from last night. She studied the puffing steamers pushing barges in jangled routes up and down the biggest river she'd seen. At the far end of the wharf, a small, bright-colored steamboat bobbed near the water's edge. Upward-curving roofs perched like pine green ladies' hats on each end of the red and orange vessel. Past the shabby wharf, against a clear morning backdrop, a locomotive towed a lone railroad car along a sweeping iron bridge. Molly walked toward the station, a colossal steel shed covering a waiting line of trains, all the trains in the world.

Venturing into the depot, Molly rested on a double-sided bench. The mob rushed through the waiting hall with the same fever as the boulevard crowd. Their gaggle of confused voices boiled up louder than the people who built the Tower of Babel. Straightening Skillet's rhinestone locket around her neck, the silt residue of lost faces tingled in her fingers, their souls shivering in the gaps of each determined traveler's ripples, like hundreds of pebbles cast into a pond. Shackled to their destinations, their currents collided like stormwater streams crashing together.

A dark-haired young woman stood in the center of the train station with a toddler at her side and a bawling baby in her arms. The woman, perhaps two or three years older than Molly, examined the train schedule, struggling not to trip over the pestering toddler cowering in her skirt. Leaning forward, she stared at the burdened mother.

"Mind your potatoes, little sister," a voice hissed from the other side of the wooden bench.

Molly pivoted to locate the stony voice, checking out the figure seated behind her and the path to the exit.

"That bird ain't on the up and up."

A short-haired woman in beige, soft-collared coveralls

crossed her arms and slid closer. "She borrows them kids from a knock shop. Claims someone stole her first-class tickets. You ain't a heel. Maybe buy her lunch, too. Lo and behold, she shares your cabbage with her girlfriend turning johns."

The young woman's baby squalled.

Molly gave the husky tipster her brisk parlor girl grin and shot out the depot door, back in the direction of the hotel.

From the tearoom on the top floor of Goldstein's Emporium, Molly had watched the steamboats ferry passengers to the amusement parks. She'd eaten cold vegetable soup and cucumber and watercress sandwiches without any crust, wondering which boat would carry her and Cotton to the picnic he'd promised once she'd agreed to play banker. Soon after her tearoom snack, she'd bought shoes from each department store she'd visited, and now, lugging her parcels, she searched for the hotel's back entrance. Toting the clunky boxes by their rough-hewn twine strained her arms. The train depot incident had made her too suspicious of the hoity-toity salesclerks to arrange for her purchases to be delivered. The late afternoon sun faded below the maze of buildings, turning the alleyway into a dusky damp chalk cave.

After sundown, her cravings grew fangs.

Molly had stopped counting the days since her last dose, dabbing at the ebbing dreamland like a trough of sweat above her lip. The aching for Madam Mercier's syringe, her sloppy ritual, burst into a wistful chant—she should have pinched the paisley satchel. Whiskey dulled the itch at first, but then inflamed it, suffocating her until she blacked out on her ass.

Male voices boomed from around the corner of the building.

Setting her bags down, Molly was still uncertain whether the waiter's real name was Clifford or Cliff and what she'd do if she couldn't find him. At her last stop, she'd scrounged up a piece of satin. She tucked scrap swab into her dress pocket.

Her calloused palms would slow the chore, if it truly came to rubbing his willie. The shiny remnant would protect from any sticky mess.

Molly approached the back entrance.

Three men huddled around an ash can.

"Cliff? Mr. Clifford?" Molly asked, unburdened by shoeboxes, the nimbleness restored to her arms.

The men turned to face her. All three wore suede vests and aprons but only two had on narrow black ties.

"I could be Clifford," the man without the tie on said.

A pair of gas sconces shined on the trio, and Molly recognized the man who'd spoken as the waiter she'd flirted with at dinner. "I ate at the English Grill last night." She edged nearer the middle of the threesome. The cigarette smoke couldn't mask the rank odor of burnt lard.

"Sure, sure, with, uh, the captain." Clifford sat down on the edge of the ash can. The other two men flicked their cigarette butts into the distance and went inside with a flash of smiles.

"Exactly, but he don't hold my sole attention." The alleyway cobblestones were bumpy and coated with watery kitchen grease. Molly worked to keep her footing sure.

"From my angle, you and the captain were having a few jollies."

"He's keen for a few laughs, but not real fun."

"Real fun?" Clifford reached for a pack of cigarettes from his inside his vest and offered one to Molly.

Sliding the cigarette out of the red pack, Molly put it between her lips, and leaned in toward Clifford. He lit a match. Molly cupped his hand, the same as the parlor girls back at the lodge, drew it to her, and held it before letting it go. Arching her neck, she blew her first puff into the air above Clifford's head. "The kind that comes from a nice friendly doctor."

Clifford pumped out a line of thick smoke rings.

"You looking for a trip to the moon?" he asked.

"A long, gentle trip."

"I know a sawbones," Clifford said, pressing the inside of his knee against her hip. Hooking his leg around her calves, Clifford pulled her closer to the dented ash can.

Molly dropped her cigarette and bound the satin swab around her fingers.

A thud whacked the other side of the door and the back entrance flew open, banging against the side of the wall. A man stormed into the alleyway.

"They said you was out here with some bird," the stout man said with the merciless mockery of an annoyed foreman uncoiling his whip. "I heard it was roarin' after I left. I trust you ain't spendin' the monies due me."

"Miller, why you gotta always be too damn loud?" Clifford let loose his hold on Molly.

Stepping away from the waiter, Molly recognized the chubby neck of the hotel detective.

"Nice bubs," Miller said, inspecting Molly.

"Simmer down."

Miller tugged at his crotch.

"For Christ sakes." Clifford slipped another smoke out of the pack.

Miller kicked the ash can out from under Clifford, toppling the waiter to the ground.

Molly shrank back toward the corner of the building.

Grabbing Clifford by his suede vest, Miller cocked his head and shouted at Molly, "Scram, before I put my brogan up that plump rump of yours."

Whirling around to run for the front door, Molly stumbled, but her clenched hand landed on the greasy cobblestones, and she righted herself, the satin swab shielding her knuckles. She snatched up her boxes and hurried to the hotel entrance. The same young boy from earlier that morning opened the door with a smile.

"Afternoon, ma'am. Can I get those bags for you?"

Molly rushed past him without a greeting or a grin.

Standing in front of the elevator was Cotton, as bleary-eyed as Skillet on a holiday bender. "Holy Methuselah, you buy something from every store on Broadway."

Thrusting her bags at his feet, Molly stashed her satin swab back in her handbag.

"We're meeting Arch for cocktails." Cotton grabbed the boxes and guided her to the elevator.

"Exactly the kick I need," Molly said, stepping on the waiting elevator. As the brass gate shut, Molly spotted the husky tipster from the train depot—with the cropped hair and tan work suit—resting against a marble pillar in the lobby. The car began to rise, and she hooked her arm inside Cotton's for the ride to their room. Next time she ventured outside the hotel without him, she'd to be certain to wear his ring.

Chapter 30

In the time it had taken Cotton to smoke a couple of cigarettes and take four sips of whiskey, before she snatched the bottle away, he'd watched Molly wash her face, change dresses twice, brush her hair, and tear open her packages. Trying on the third pair of her new shoes, she stood in front of the mirror holding out one foot and pointing her toes.

"Snazzy," Cotton said from the armchair in the corner, mustering as much conviction as he could. He'd like the square stacked heel on the first pair more—it reminded him of Havana. Her slender calves were tan and taught. The next time she took off shopping, he'd join her and find a pair of silk stockings to accent her legs.

Scowling at Cotton, Molly kicked off her shoes and slipped on the first pair she'd modeled. She downed the last drop of whiskey and tossed the empty pint bottle underhand to him.

"Whoa." Cotton caught the bottle as it floated toward his chest.

Molly carried the shopping bag that served as her suitcase bag to the edge of the bed, sat down, and opened the night-stand drawer. Taking out an irregular cut piece of cloth from her handbag, she hunched over the drawer and fiddled with the Bible.

There were six-hundred-and-eighty dollars hidden in the tenth chapter of Luke, between the Mission of the Seventy and their Return. After he'd been unable to find her in any of the department stores, Cotton had read the story and counted the money, several times.

Molly stuffed a bundle into her handbag, buried the Bible in her shopping bag, and stood up.

"We having supper?" she asked, putting on Cotton's lucky

ring with a slight shimmy in her hips.

"We're already on the tail edge of cocktail hour." Cotton pushed himself up from the leather armchair and checked his appearance in the floor mirror. The sleek maroon bundle was a good sign. "We could sample a starter at the English Grill," he said, combing his hair with his fingers then tightening his tie snug around his collar.

"Too many creepy hay burners eyeballing me," Molly giggled. "Do you think I'll need my sweater?"

Cotton picked up her cardigan sweater from the back of the vanity chair and held it out for her.

"I hope your pal has tidbits to nibble on," Molly said, stepping nearer to him.

Cotton draped the blue-green cardigan over her slinky shoulders. After a couple of more pops, he'd hem her up in the corner of the suite and coax her back to the bedroom. His old chum would understand a quick need for privacy.

Chapter 31

Arch poured the last drops from the cocktail shaker into her glass. "Cap, this lady loves Manhattans. You should take her." He set the silver shaker on the tray and slumped back in the in the chair opposite her and Cotton on the sofa.

Dangling her shoe at the end of her foot, Molly sipped the red violet drink, relishing the slivers of ice cooling the burn of the bourbon.

"On my way up to Saratoga, I'm staying over at this nouveau uptown spot overlooking the park. You two come along."

"I'll lead the charge." Molly let loose a silly titter of laughs and uncrossed her legs. The hem of her peach dress rose above her knees.

"Been a long time since I was that far north," Cotton said, shifting his untouched glass of whiskey from one hand to the other.

"Great town for the freshly gilded seeking people to clean their money." Arch sat upright in his club chair.

"That's a chore I never imagined—scrubbing and sweeping money," Molly said, enjoying a small taste of her cocktail, leaving her thighs parted. She'd attracted Cotton's attention earlier, and now his pal was staring at her well-turned legs. It wasn't the first evening she'd held the interest of two men at once—during the madam's auctions she'd captivated the entire crowd—but now was the first time their focus kindled a flutter. Like her, and all the guests that staggered through the lodge, both men were inclined to lust. They were all fornicators. "So playing cards and cleaning money, that's your talent?"

"You remind me of this flick I caught the other night," he

replied, shaking his head. "If your hair was bobbed short, you could have been the star—Clara Bow."

Molly crossed her legs towards Arch.

"She played this sales gal, Betty Lou I think her name was. It's playing around the corner at the Majestic."

"What about those iron beasts?" Cotton said loud and fast, in one long word.

"Iron beasts?" Molly asked.

"A steam shovel manufacturer up in Milwaukee." Arch said. "Honestly, the Italians in that town are more practical than the Chicago outfit. It's the goddamn headstrong Bolshevik bastards that require the patience of saints. Give me the sign, Cap, and I'll arrange for you to land a plum sales territory."

"Ain't we gonna traverse the globe?" Molly knocked Cotton's shoulder with hers. "Rail cars with silver tea service and ocean liner staterooms with private balconies?"

"I'm your butler this evening, and my position requires serving you a plate of canapes." Jumping up from the sofa, Cotton walked to the serving cart in the corner of the suite.

Molly tilted closer to Arch, leaning into the center of the coffee table between them. "First, he liquors me up. Then, he tells me to eat. Who knows what he'll want me to do next?"

"Come over and I'll tell you precisely what I'm figuring to do," Cotton said, like a randy barker corralling passers-by.

"Throw an extra couple of pieces on her plate," Arch shouted over his shoulder, reclining back in his seat. "Resuscitate us with toasted ravioli and pastry puffs."

"Too late for tidbits," Molly purred like a tipsy cat. Lowering her eyes, she checked to make sure her purse was safe on the floor. The potent mixed drinks made the cream-colored walls drift to-and-fro, but the four-hundred dollars wrapped in the satin swab worked as a ballast.

Cotton handed her a napkin and a golden-baked triangle with green cream oozing out the sides.

"Nope, nope, nope." Molly pursed her lips shut, her flutter evaporating.

"You need the powder room?" Cotton asked, plopping the dainty pastry back on the plate.

"I'm as comfortable as a magnolia in the silvery moon."

"You're welcome to use the facilities in the bedroom," Arch said.

Cotton stuck out his hand.

"Who all is playing tonight?" Molly asked, snickering at his advancing palm.

"Fellas you probably don't wanna know."

Cotton's carny tone had disappeared, replaced with the scolding nag of the shop clerks who'd sneered at her sandals. He sat back down on the sofa next to her, his hand retreating to his lap.

"How are my man's odds on winning?"

"The captain is luckier than a buggy full of Irishmen. Don't fret. You're wearing his lucky ring."

"Risk a fortune on a scrawny ring?" Molly heard herself resurrect her mother's sniping doubt.

"Your stakes all set?" Arch asked his old army pal.

"This is like when that stint we did at that crumbling station near El Paso, between the Federales and the Villistas. We had all the mescal. And all the puta. Guaranteed."

"No harm in relinquishing your seat."

"I'm good for the seat," Cotton said, his flinty gaze returning.

At the start of a boundless row of tobacco plants—festering with budworms, more work calling and the daylight dying out—Molly had seen her father with the identical firm jaw and fixed eyes. Alma Mae had fettered her thoughts to stinginess, binding her to an ungenerous prison. Skillet never abandoned his faith in their year of jubilee. Molly picked her handbag off the floor and tucked it next to her.

Cotton pointed his body at Molly, moving his arm to the

cushion behind her neck. Bending toward her, he kissed her cheek.

The press of his lips against her skin tingled. She didn't dare trust the frivolous quiver expanding in her chest. Cotton had carried her away from Scots Station, saved her from Hinton, but she'd overheard loads of cocky liars brag about the birds they killed, the parlor girls they pleased, and the big-dollar pots they'd won in the poker room. She could find other men, other kisses, and other liars. Although, backing away would be the unbeliever's path. Busting out demanded courage. Having her year of jubilee was a test of fortitude. He couldn't lose all her money. She opened her handbag, plunked the satin swab of money down on the coffee table, and stood up. "I'd love another one of those Manhattans."

"Though she be but little, she's fierce," Arch said with an unsure drop-jaw smile.

"And sassy." Cotton scooped up the maroon swab and put the sleek bundle of money in his suit coat pocket.

Chapter 32

The dwarf grandfather clock in the Broadway suite was soon to strike four a.m., and the penthouse chambers were noxious with the bite of cigars and foot odor. Lucius Arnold would've long ago ordered his men to douse the campfire and kennel the hounds, but he never would've gotten into a card game with Monk Houlihan and Big Billy Bigelow. Cotton peeked at his cards for the third or fourth time. The snoring L&N railroad man was slouched sideways in his seat; he'd folded a half-dozen hands in a row.

"Thought you old doughboys knew how to play, Archibald?" Monk Houlihan said, twirling his whiskers, the left and then the right, rotating them between his manicured fingertips.

Cotton had noticed Houlihan playing with his mustache several times throughout the evening. The skinny Irishman could be grooming himself or accidentally signaling his cards, confidence or doubt. Cotton peeked at his own cards one more time—trip sixes.

"Sure we do," Arch said, rearing back from the table. "It's like, I don't know." He gave Cotton, his former battalion comrade, the same series of narrow blinks as he did when their major dispensed his baffling orders. They both knew slow-paying Houlihan and Big Billy was a sucker strategy. "Maybe riding a horse."

Two or three hours ago, Cotton had lost the four-hundred-dollar stake Molly had given him. Arch had loaned him fifty bucks, and had mentioned the sales territory in Milwaukee. He'd gotten down to three red chips, but winning one deal at a time was the only way to get it back. He claimed two nice thirty-dollar pots with only a pair and needed this hand to maintain his lucky streak. Rubbing his throbbing jaw, Cotton counted the kitty—sixty. "I'm in for twenty-five," he said, tossing in his bet, running up the pot.

Big Billy Bigelow peered at the five red chips like they were the last morsels of the Benedictine sandwich platter he'd eaten at midnight. His tongue nudged out between his lips, and he matched the twenty-five dollar bet without wasting a word.

"Now we're cooking," Houlihan said with an eager bop. "No-limits raise?"

"Ab-so-lute-lee." Bigelow smacked his plump lips.

"Sure," Cotton said. They'd been raising the limit all night, and each time it had served to increase the rate of his loses, but now he'd snagged the skinny Irishman in his own snare.

"Atta boy, no holds barred." Houlihan dropped five reds into the pot, and then flung five blue chips into the center of the table. He rotated his waxy red whiskers between his thumbs.

Two floors down, Molly was asleep, waiting for him. They should've been curled together, but he couldn't arrive back in bed without some of her stake intact. Before the game, he'd given her a BC powder and tucked her in bed. Tomorrow, he'd nurse her hangover with a champagne picnic out to the falls. They'd roll around naked in the sunshine with no mention of the iron beast being their future. Cotton pitched in his in five blue chips and stacked up his leftover chips, four reds and five whites. A hunger pang roiled his insides. He tossed his remaining stake onto the heap.

"Any of you fellas know of a good oyster joint?" Big Billy plopped his cards down on the table and waved off the raise with his sallow fist. The rumor was he'd never been seen outdoors in the daytime.

"I was bound for the Chinaman's steamer. But I know a night-owl spot along the way," Houlihan said. "Captain, I ain't counting all 'dem chips, but it appears you called with twenty-five." He set five reds chips on top of the pile. "Let's see who's leaving with heartache and who's leaving with love." The skinny Irishmen laid out his hand. "Two pair, aces and eights—a dead man's hand."

Cotton slapped his playing cards onto the table. "The devil takes a dead man, trip sixes,"

"Satan appears." Houlihan stood up from the table. "Time for this brokenhearted Irish boy to cash 'em out."

Cotton calculated his winnings—two-hundred-and-sixty-five dollars—but Houlihan had more of Molly's money left to recover. "You aren't letting me, or the devil, run you off?"

"I'm in mind to be battling the slant-eyed demon on the *Shanghai Dragon*," Houlihan said, straightening his bowtie. "Mend my heartache with a bang of the gong."

"What's a couple more hands to a top dog?" Cotton said, cajoling him with the same fervor he'd coaxed Molly for the stake.

"I don't care to match your hefty pot in a final game—one card gut." The skinny Irishmen brushed the sleeves of his suit coat. "Top dog takes all."

Rocking back from the poker table, Cotton scanned the jumbled collection of blue, red, and white chips. His gaze darted over to his old chum. "Lieutenant deals?"

A creased brow accompanied Arch's rapid blinking.

Houlihan answered by stacking two black chips, an orange chip, and a shamrock-green one next to the mishmash prize.

Cotton's knee jerked up and down under the table.

After shuffling the deck, Arch extended it to Big Billy. "You care for the honor of cutting?"

"If it gets me closer to beer and oysters." Bigelow picked up the deck with one hand, held it between his sausage fingers, slipped the top half over his thumb, and slid the bottom half to the top. He set the deck in front of the lieutenant.

Arch dealt one card face down to each gambler.

"I'd offer you the chance to raise, but I don't think you have in ya." Gripping the edge of the table with both hands, Houlihan hunched over his lone card. "Age before beauty."

Cotton flicked his card over. "One-eyed Jack." A scoundrel's unbroken black moxie. "And a spade to boot."

The skinny Irishmen plucked his card up and flung it down on the tabletop.

The melancholy gloom of the Suicide King pierced Cotton's grit.

"Woof-woof growled the wolfhound." Monk Houlihan raked the winnings into his jacket pocket. "Big Billy, my heart and my cash have been restored. I'm buying the buckets of beers and pails of oysters. You boys from the Lost Battalion want to join in? I'll lead the way."

"We weren't lost, the Huns founds us plenty," Arch replied.

From the far corner, the grandfather clock sounded at the top of the hour.

Turning away from the table, Cotton flinched at each measured strike.

Sitting on the tile floor next to the bathtub, Cotton thought Molly's maroon shopping bag resembled an orphan. He had brought it with him into the bathroom after he stumbled on it sneaking into their room. Rather than flop about in the bed, he'd stretched out in the tub. Sleep would be a struggle. Passing out wasn't an option. He wasn't drunk. His head was bursting. The foundling bag, like a vagrant child in the middle of an ivory cobblestone street, begged him not to squander his schooling. Tonight's game was an education, a reconnaissance mission. He'd learned the lesson of not snaring yourself in your own trap. Now, he knew to push ahead when Houlihan twirled his whiskers, and that Bigelow was apt to make mistakes if he was hungry. Cotton leaned up and pulled the shopping bag into the tub. Glancing at the bathroom door, he listened—only the bellow of ship horns starting the workday on the river. Scouring past her new wardrobe, he recalled seeing several more fifty-dollar bills tucked in Luke's Gospel. Last night had been the ante. Tonight, the numbers would be in his favor. He ransacked his way to the bottom, but only found dresses and underclothes. He dumped the bulky shopping bag over in the tub. She'd taken out the Bible. Rescinded her confidence. Stuffing her clothes back in the shopping bag, he left it stranded in the empty bathtub.

As Cotton slipped into bed, Molly raised her hand, and he grabbed it, dozing off before his headache could torture him further.

For more information about The Lost Battalion, subscribe to Southern Fried Karma's YouTube channel, Fugitive Views.

Chapter 33

Molly crouched on the side of a steep ravine. Rose huddled alongside her. Between the grim gaps in the treetops, a bleached moon spied on the forest. A pack of wolves lurked on the boundary, feeding on the piles of rotting corpses. The sloping sides of the gulch formed a pouch, a wooded pocket of the earth. *Help me*, a voice pleaded. From the early fall chill, a twisting pain soaked her knees, and the back of her calves burned. She crawled away from Rose towards the begging voice, to the darkest edge. With each movement, the black mud clutched at her. Loose strands of barbed wire, the wolf's razor claws, thrashed above her head. *Captain Arnold.* And now the gaunt voice had hollow eyes and a bandaged face cradled in her hands. With a certainty that came from toiling months and miles, Molly knew this was Corporal Harrison, and his garbled message never ceased calling from a hazy distant field. *Chicago. Down in Little Hell, near West Oak Street. Ain't no daggone whore. Gabrielle gotta get my pay.*

Rose grabbed Molly's leg, yanking her away as Harrison melted into the sea of dreams.

Chapter 34

A sharp twitch jolted her leg, jarring Molly awake. Cotton's hand rested below her navel, and she pulled it in close to her breasts. The dream of the hollow-eyed soldier wasn't hers—but she wasn't an intruder. Harrison had pursued her. Rose had guided her.

In front of the hotel, the trolley cars screeched, clanking up and down the rousing street. Today, Cotton was taking her over to the falls for a champagne picnic. He'd get fresh after he got her tipsy. In bed now, his crotch was pressed neatly up against her hips, cozy and warm. Despite his promise not to get drunk at the card game last night, he'd stumbled in and retreated to the bathroom. Back at the lodge, she'd overheard guests at the breakfast table swear off Hinton's corn liquor only to show up in the parlor that evening drunker than they were the night before. Cotton would wake up thirsty for ice water and ready to fuck. She'd make him wait, nudging her ass against his morning erection. He'd brag about his winnings at the poker table, hoping she'd let him squeeze in more than the tip. But first, she needed to freshen up. She wriggled out from under his arm and went into the bathroom.

Perched on the indoor toilet seat, imagining soaking in a bubble bath before their picnic, she saw her Woolworth's bag in the tub. She clamped her thighs together and grabbed the shopping bag, tumbling through it to see if anything was missing. The clothes she'd folded were jumbled wads. Her silk slip was buried on the bottom crammed next to her scarf. It wasn't the redheaded colored maid that she needed to worry about. A flush of water ran through the pipes in the wall. The bedroom was still quiet. First thing this morning, she'd buy herself a decent travel suitcase with a lock. Molly snatched her robe off the hook and swung the bathroom door open so hard it banged the doorstep. She raised the blinds, plopped down into the lounge chair, and picked up the telephone.

With a groan, Cotton pulled the pillow over his head.

"What you want from room service?" Molly asked as if she was truly a giddy bride on her honeymoon. "I'm getting bacon and pecan waffles with extra whipped butter."

"What in tarnation?" Cotton's shouts were muffled by the pillow.

"Hopefully that handsome waiter I saw in the coffee shop will bring it." Molly peeled the robe off one shoulder, exposing her breast. "You think he'd like my slinky satin robe to come off a teensy bit?"

"Have you lost your country-ass backward Alabama mind?"

"It ain't my mind I lost."

Cotton sat up in bed, the pillow across his stomach like a puffy shield. "It's not lost. I know right where to find it."

"Do tell?" Molly said, covering herself.

"Monk Houlihan has most of it, but I'll win it all back from the scrawny Mick tonight, plus some."

"What're you figuring to do? Conk him over the head? Be his cream-puff?"

"You learn all these shenanigans at the madam's harlot boarding school back in Perry County?" Cotton waved his hand in the air. "Business partners shouldn't be slandering shrews."

"You rummage through my Woolworth's?"

"Best to consider it an initial investment."

"Ha, one thing I did learn in Perry County was not to sow good seed on bad land. How much did you lose to this Houlihan fella?"

"You can't run off with money on the table."

"Running off might be the smartest move. How much of my money is this lanky whatever holding?"

"Hold your water. It's guaranteed to be better tonight."

"Are you daffy? Still drunk? Don't ever talk about folks from Alabama being slow."

"All told, four-fifty."

Plunking the receiver back in the cradle, Molly scanned the room. Hinton's Colt .45 was locked in the trunk of the car, but the lamp next to the bed would serve as good as an ax handle. Molly would bet that's the weapon Alma Mae would pick—settling their argument with a few swift whacks from the purple and green electric lamp. Her mother wouldn't care a lick about involving the hotel detective and having them both go to jail. While Madam Mercier would pick at Cotton's guilt like a scab, pleasuring herself on controlling him with his shame, and then she'd get shed of him, a locomotive unbuckling and hitching up with a new car as soon it was opportune. "Can you even pay the hotel bill?"

"Can we?" Cotton said, his voice matching Harrison's lifeless expression.

Molly pushed herself up and out of the lounge chair. "I don't care to shake the dust off my new shoes and never come back to the Brown Hotel."

"I can't leave a man behind with a debt unpaid."

Stepping closer to the bed, Molly could see Cotton's scrunched face, the stark morning light crushing him. It was the same crumpled look her father couldn't disguise. "How much do you owe Archibald?"

"Fifty dollars."

"Hmm, you planning on paying me back with this big sales job? Where's it at?"

"Milwaukee, up north. Wisconsin."

"Is that anywhere near Chicago?"

"It can be."

"Marshall Fields?"

"I'll drive you right down Michigan Avenue past the Wrigley building with the top down like you're in a ticker-tape parade." Cotton tossed the pillow to the side. "I'm telling you, steam shovels are revolutionizing the world. I could pay you back promptly. I'd venture they'll offer me a draw against future commission."

Molly cinched her robe tight around her waist and paced the room.

"But that's the type of question I'd have to ask the main executive fellow in person—gentleman to gentleman."

"Any other army buddies along the way?" Molly asked, taking a final look out the hotel window. Giving him money to pay Archibald was securing an ally, but she didn't ask to be a dead soldier's messenger. Most likely, she'd overheard Cotton and his old army buddy swapping war stories, and the rest of the dream could've come from anywhere, newsreels she'd seen long ago. Gazing down at the rushing city folks, she couldn't separate the wheat from the tares.

"None we need to worry over, but I need to get square with Arch."

"I'm drawing a hot bath and soaking myself in some bubbles and perfumed water." Turning away from the casement window, Molly took the Bible from the nightstand drawer, and headed toward the bathroom.

"Are we having our champagne picnic?" Cotton asked, wringing his hands together.

Molly paused at the threshold. "How good you know this Monk?"

"First time I played cards with him, but he leaves his mark—the cocky, natty type."

"Where's he lodging at?"

"I assume the Seelbach. Arch would know. Why?"

"'Cause, no scrawny bastard lays hold of what I earned." Molly said, leaning up against the doorframe, posing with one foot on the carpet and one on the chilly tile floor. Wiggling out of her robe, she crossed all the way into the bathroom, closed the door, and locked it shut.

Chapter 35

Encountering fickle young girls numbed Cotton, but he couldn't deaden the pressure in his bladder. For an hour or so, long enough for the narrow hallway to grow loud with hotel guests fiddling with their room keys, he listened through the bathroom door. He'd heard Molly running the bath—which primed his urge to piss. At times, she'd hummed "Jesus Loves Me," mixed with a string of Negro blues tunes while she soaked, and he'd caught the slippery squeak of her stepping out of the tub to dry herself.

Cotton tapped on the sealed bathroom door. "There's a backup in my boiler room."

A refrain of rapid humming returned.

"Please," he added, knocking again.

The lock clicked.

The door cracked open.

As Cotton entered, Molly swept past, lips closed, warbling. The silky sleeve of her robe skimmed his side.

"Thanks much," he said, grateful for not having to hunt up the room key or threaten to use it. Passing water in the dewy bathroom satisfied him more than usual, but he couldn't afford for his daily piss routine to be the best part of his day.

Returning to the bedroom, Molly was seated at the dressing table, gripping his pocket knife in one hand and a clump of hair in the other. "Geezus hell, you scalped yourself," Cotton said with a sharp cry, taking a step back before moving next to her.

"That stung," she said, laying down the buck brown knife on top of the cluttered vanity. Molly's shoulders drooped, and she gazed at the mass of rough-cut wet hair like a child who'd plucked a patch of daisies and discovered the roots.

"If I'd known you wanted a fresh coiffure, I'd have scrounged you up a pair of scissors, not a blade too dull to cut goat cheese."

"I'm aiming at bob cutting it anyway."

Cotton scratched his unshaven jaw, deciding whether he was sharing a foxhole with a crackpot. "As hairdressers go, you're more of a butcher."

Molly sat up straight on the padded bench seat. "I need a new dress. Not a dull five and dime smock. A high-dollar gown with shimmering embroidery and frilly fringe."

"Simple enough," he said. The modern style evening gowns were made for buxom bodies like hers, for the rise of Molly's bosoms above the plunging V-neck line and the silhouette of her hips swaying under chiffon and sparkling beads. "What else you figuring?"

"Heading to the Seelbach, right after dark, around cocktail time," she said with the cockiness of every sportsman planning a hunt.

Cotton picked up his pocket knife and folded the blade back. His father would classify Molly as a gullible wench deceived by her own hysteria, but she was high ground to fall back on and square it with Arch to at least land the steam shovel job. Abandoning her would banish him to some mill town somewhere in Ohio, or Indiana, selling some kind of cornfield implement to cow patty cranks. "You need a companion to protect you?"

"For tonight, I'm Maggie." She curled the cluster of sheared locks around her fingers. "Better yet, you call me Margaret."

"However you like, but as your partner, I recommend wearing a hat 'til we find you a hair-dresser."

Chapter 36

Pursuing a stag Irishman was simpler than tracking a white-tail buck. They rutted often, taverns were their habitat, and boisterous grunts and bellows their mating calls. Before she saw Monk Houlihan at the Seelbach Hotel, Molly heard his jovial hoots streaming from an alcove in the hotel bar. She would've preferred a moment to study the crowd and the bar's layout, to get comfortable on her stool. But when she walked by alone, Irish Monk and his tablemates paused their card game and one of them whistled, a high-pitched leering call that resounded through the vast marble arches of the Oakroom.

Seated at the end of the wooden bar, Molly was skimming the menu when the slender red-head approached her.

"I'd recommend the grilled sardines," Houlihan said, straddling the far edge of the stool to the left of her.

Glancing up, Molly flicked him a curt smile and returned to the snack menu. His deep rowdy voice and quick accent jarred her ears, adding a seesaw-like feeling to the long varnished bar.

"But the Scotch eggs aren't too awfully bad for a starter. Which may sound off the face comin' from the likes of me, but we was all bog jumpers at some point." Houlihan tweaked the upward curve of his mustache and slipped closer to Molly. "Besides, my ma' was a Kraut."

Without raising her eyes, Molly grinned. She detected his scent. It reminded her of the madam's lusty smell late in the afternoon after her morning spritz of gardenia perfume had faded. Not a sour funk, but the smoldering scent of a heated casting, which diminished after a dose.

"So what'll you have? Orangeade? Fruit punch?" Houlihan asked, waving the bartender over to their end of the bar.

"I'm waiting for my cousin to join me," Molly said, fingering the chain of Rose's rhinestone locket, her amulet, the same as Sally's twisted totems hanging from her backwoods cabin. Pivoting away from him, Molly glanced at the door. Her bar stool teetered on the uneven tile floor. She'd left Cotton in the lobby as a lookout, drinking coffee and reading the evening paper. She turned back to face Houlihan and smiled again, short and bashful. "He's all balled up with traveling stress."

The bartender walked down to their end of the bar.

"A couple of those mint drinks, Jimmy, the kind with the juniper water," Houlihan said, holding up two fingers.

"Juniper water?" Molly asked after the barkeep left to fix their cocktails.

"A gin mint fizz, sweeter than that sour mash rotgut," he replied.

The stout barkeep sat the drinks in front of them.

Houlihan raised his glass. "May the devil cut the toes off your foes."

Molly giggled and clinked glasses. She tasted her cocktail; the earthy sweetness reminded her of candy-coated pine needles. It didn't have the cloying burn of the whiskey Cotton drank straight from the bottle. She sipped it again.

Pulling a cigar from his inside pocket, Houlihan sparked a match head with his fingernail.

Molly took a long, fast drink of her cocktail. The sparkly libation settled her nerves but stirred her cravings.

"Not bad is it?" he asked between puffs of his squat cigar.

"Too divine." Shifting in her stool, Molly angled her legs in the slender Irishman's direction.

"I'll have to order us another round before your chaperone arrives." Houlihan said, snapping his fingers at the overworked barkeep. "Montgomery Houlihan." He dipped his head and hoisted his glass, his yellow-green eyes flaring like the sun breaking through a patchwork of leafy woods. "Born somewhere between Berlin and Belfast. Most often found chasing the horizon." The Irishman snuck his arm around the back of her bar stool.

"Margaret, Margaret Mercier, I was a nursing student in Atlanta, but I guess now I'm a stranded traveler."

"Cheers."

Like the madam had schooled the parlor girls, she chatted with Houlihan like a couple at an ice cream social, using the lie about her family perishing in the tornado to disarm him. He told her that the Spanish flu had claimed his wife and two children, so he left for America to avoid troubles. Molly brushed his arm and laughed at his bawdy jokes as she'd been instructed.

"So what difficulties you having that's got your cousin late for drinks?" Houlihan asked.

"Truth be told, some floozy pickpocketed him smack-dab in the center of the terminal."

"The craven will stoop low when they're desperate. Sorry for your worries," he said, tipping his glass. "Where are you headed?"

"Milwaukee, for a nursing position," Molly replied in her thick drawl like a student struggling to recite a history lesson.

"Good on you." The Irishmen moved his arm off her stool, draping it across her back. "You working at the Catholic children's hospital down by the iron millworks or the Jesuit charity clinic near the brewery?"

"The children's one, it's been the Lord's calling since I lost my own little brother," she said, glimpsing her reflection in the wall-length mirror behind the bar. Lying was as easy as shopping for a different wardrobe. Since she first slipped on her new outfit, she'd been admiring her fancy gold dress and bob cut hairdo in the hotel room's cheval glass. In storefront windows along the walk to the Seelbach, she viewed her glittering image as a fresher version of the parlor girls. If they were a couple courting after Sunday church, he was the awkward widower panting over the pretty orphan girl.

"St. Brigit?"

"Yes, sir." Molly focused on the moist rim of her cocktail glass.

"The problem with that town is the open sewer running through the middle and the greasy Wops grifters and pinko Polacks in charge. But I ain't never been." The Irishmen squeezed her bare shoulders. "Are you always a good girl?"

Resisting the instinct to shrink from his grasp pressing her upper arm, Molly drained the rest of her second mint fizz.

"I'm not in the habit of paying for what most heifers will hand out for nothing," Houlihan tightened his hug around Molly, "but I might for fresh sweet cream such as yours."

All her money was in her handbag, Gabe's twenty dollars.

"I'm game to splurge on a nice romp with a keen gal."

Cotton's car was packed.

"How's twenty dollars for a hearty steak and a chance to bang the gong?"

"You're full of wild notions." Molly could worm off with an offended gasp.

"The black tar sends you floating into the mystic seas."

Spotting a big buck was simple, but after you've taken your shot, you still needed to retrieve your kill, pursue your wounded quarry. "Better than a friendly doctor?" Molly asked. If the Lord allowed a holiday turkey hunt to lead her to a Hinton's whorehouse and then a wobbly barstool days away from Scots Station, she could never be certain where any choice would have her land. Yet picking a dose required little faith. Her only prayer need be *Jesus don't let me die tonight. Don't let me drown crossing the river.*

"You hip for the *Shanghai Dragon?*"

With a smooth motion, Molly slid her hand below the bar, and worked her fingers across Houlihan's thigh. "Fifty— without the dinner." She tugged at his crotch this same as the plastered parlor girls were doing with beneath the painting of the picnickers in the meadow. Wistful memories of their pale red cheeks rang out like a schoolyard bell, lounging all day in silky nightclothes, Marie razzing poor Sally with her mail-order heat massager, and Viola and Pearl farting out loud until they soiled their underdrawers. The madam would mean to recoup all her cash plus a healthy gratuity for good measure.

Houlihan flung a five-dollar bill down on the bar top. "You are a sporty lass."

"And we only just met," Molly said, spotting Monk's overstuffed wallet.

"I'd normally hustle a stroller in and out of the side door, but for an orphaned nursing student, we'll be using the lobby."

Chapter 37

The bizarre headline in the Saturday evening edition of the *Louisville Courier-Journal* concerned Cotton: "Television Now a Reality; Secretary Hoover Beamed from DC to NYC." He'd read the article twice, and still didn't fully understand the benefit of sending images over phone lines. Herbert Hoover's frumpy mug was unpleasant enough on the front page of a nickel newspaper—it wasn't a scientific achievement to compel folks to listen and watch him both. He set the newspaper down, picked up his whiskey-spiked coffee, and wondered would it be like to transmit moving pictures of Molly in the Oakroom to him in the Seelbach's lobby.

Back at the Brown, Cotton had tried to advise Molly on what to do if she found Monk. He'd watch her fiddle with her suspender belt and suggested that she not follow through with her wild notions. But she went about rolling up her beige silk stockings and hooking them to her lace garter. For a young girl, Molly was full-grown. Cotton figured they bred country gals that way in Scots Stations. Her forearms were solid. Her taut thighs ample enough to generate a hearty kick to the cocky bastard's groin. But most any man, especially an angry Irishman, could overpower her unless she caught them by surprise. They rejected the idea of bringing pistols along. Neither of them thought of toting Hinton's shiny Colt .45 to the Seelbach was smart—too many questions if the hotel detective or the city police became involved. Besides, Molly had proved clever at improvising a weapon.

A burst of crowd noise rushed from the barroom door.

Monk and Molly, her cropped auburn hair still turning eyes, strolled out of The Oakroom as cheery as a prom couple.

Snatching up his newspaper, Cotton's face knotted

together in a hot flush. At sunset on the boulevard, they'd walked down from the Brown, and Molly had reminded him that she wasn't counting on him following too close, which was satisfactory to him. He couldn't abide by the image of standing in the hallway, listening to Houlihan's vulgar grunts outside their door. He clenched the crumpled evening paper tighter, twisting it like a dying quail's neck. If Molly wouldn't change the plan, he would. After they'd taken the elevator up to his room, he'd lag behind. Knock on Monk's hotel room door with some hayseed accent. Strong arm the skinny twit when he answered. He glanced over to see the line for the elevator.

As he looked back to find the couple, he spotted Monk tipping the doorman and the twosome sauntering towards a waiting taxi. Springing up from his post in the lobby, Cotton abandoned his empty coffee cup and wadded headlines and chased after the jovial pair.

Chapter 38

Traveling through the honking snarl of Saturday night traffic, Molly felt the waddling pedestrians jammed on the sidewalks staring at the blazing yellow sedan with the black and white diamond border. Their fixed eyes were creeks that feed the river, an almighty current flowing from the mountains to the seas. Each of the upright passersby spread news of her destination to the Great Deeps of Heaven. Bristling against the rough clefts in the split leather, she squirmed in the backseat. There had to be a comfortable spot away from their sober glares and a safe distance from Houlihan's trained grip on her and her handbag

The parlor girls had gossiped about gals who tricked in cabs, riding around all night long for quick sucks and fucks. Not long after their car eased away from the curb, the slender Irishman kissed her, clasping a tuft of her new hairdo and moving her closer. The madam believed the cab's confined backseat riled up men, the locomotion, and the driver's side glance. Houlihan's roving hand landed on the back of her calf and inched up her leg with a feathery touch. Molly clamped her knees together. Back at the lodge, the madam and the girls had also blabbed about opium, mourning the rarity of the pleasure and the thrill of the mad sex that came after smoking from the pipe. The conversation would then veer into reports of opium bowls and long-stemmed pipes the parlor girls had puffed on, and from there, it was soon into racy accounts about tallywhackers. Madam Mercier had said the wicked high lifted her places the needle couldn't climb. Molly wondered if the madam had ever hopped on the *Shanghai Dragon*, but she knew Alma Mae had never seen a paddle wheeler. Never ventured past her midwife tinctures and sorcerer's potions. Sporting with Whip could have brought her mother pleasure or been another chore, no different than slaughtering a billy-goat and boiling his skinned carcass. There was no true place for her mother and Stanley in her mind. No spot where she could find them. Skillet rested in Hinton's pit, but the Lingo's cabin, their slanted family shack, was vacant. She couldn't bring herself to ponder where her little brother slept now.

Brushing his lips across her neck, Houlihan worked to wiggle his nimble hand between her clenched thighs.

With a sigh, Molly arched her back and guided him under her dress. Allowing his mouth to goad her body, she shut her eyes, sealing herself in a closet. A vibrating shape approached beneath the darkness. Like the evening star on a bright spring night, a young woman appeared in her mind, a long black braid draped over her shoulder. Her pale face like a waning humpback moon. On an instinct, as strong as her heartbeat, Molly sensed she was Monk's departed bride. The source of the impulse was as deep-rooted as the winter wind. It could have been the only birthright she could claim from her kin, or like Eve, the day had come for Molly to disobey the Lord. The serpent's sporting crafts, the wisdom of the doses, made her like God. From behind the apparition, four or five more women—each fairer, darker, or warmer—loomed liked untended pilgrims cropping up from a gloomy fog. Their faces were blanketed in a shrunken pallor.

The taxicab lurched to a halt, and Houlihan bit down on her exposed nipple, and the specters fled as soon as the sting of his teeth opened her eyes.

Monk rolled back to his side of the cab, adjusting the buttons on his fly. "You got my furnace stoked."

Molly tucked her breasts back in her dress and straightened her locket. She wrapped the hand bag's strap around her palm, the brass chain digging into her flesh. The passageway to the ship was lit with lanterns. She'd noticed Cotton lurking in the lobby, but she couldn't be troubled to guess if he'd trailed her or not. The pinkish yellow glow of the paper lamps called her, like angels inviting her up the rickety gangplank.

Chapter 39

After the doorman guided the yellow cab into a break in the boulevard traffic, Cotton charged out the lobby door.

"Hey, boy," Cotton said, advancing toward the natty doorman. "Where was that cab headed?"

"Excuse me, sir?" he replied.

"Where'd you send those two?"

"I don't rightly recall, sir." His response was as distinct as a cadet on the drill field. He stepped away from Cotton and resumed his duty, opening the door for a group of incoming guests.

Cotton studied the doorman. His topcoat and trousers were clean and pressed sharper than his full-dress uniform had been back in military college, and he wasn't a teenager like Cotton had assumed. He was closer to his own age. They'd had black troops in France, or Cotton had heard of them in combat anyway. They'd fought alongside the French Army, and the Germans had given a colored infantry regiment the nickname "Hellfighters." After Armistice Day, they'd paraded up 5th Avenue.

"I'm supposed to meet them for dinner," Cotton said, drawing near the doorman again. Molly had given him money to pay back Archie and few extra dollars for walking around money. Most nights, he wouldn't give a darkie a dime for hailing him a cab, but he pictured Monk converging on Molly in the backseat. "Can you help a soldier out?" Cotton slipped him two bucks.

The doorman pocketed the dough. "*Shanghai Dragon.*"

Cotton retreated from the Seelbach's front door. He'd heard Big Billy, or Monk, mention the floating opium brothel the other night, but he thought it was only a gambler's legend.

If he was planning on storming a paddle wheeler, he needed more whiskey and his revolver from his car back at the Brown.

Zig-zagging through the testy drivers, he caught sight of a figure down the street weaving across the traffic, too. The jaywalker trailed behind him a half a block as Cotton rushed back to the Brown. He owed the hotel over two-hundred dollars, well past his usual credit limit, and the front desk had left him several urgent messages. The house detective had to be on the watch for them skipping out on the charges. After they'd loaded up the La Salle, he'd left it in the hotel's cramped parking lot, so not to concern Miller, but there was no time to scout out the car first. Once he retrieved his pistol and his pint bottle, he'd move it around the corner near the Majestic. The movie theater crowd would give him cover. Slowing his gait, Cotton closed in on the LaSalle.

"Mister, you dropped something?" said a low and harsh voice behind him.

Retrieving the keys from his pocket, Cotton turned around. A burly shape neared him holding out their arm.

"I found your wallet." Their tone turned graceful and higher pitched.

"Don't think so," Cotton said, patting his coat pocket.

"Yep, you're right," they said, charging him and ramming their forearm into his temple.

Staggering backward, Cotton's backside smacked into the LaSalle's trunk rack. He surged at his attacker, but was met with a knee driven into his groin. He buckled over, his ball sack throbbing.

Cotton shook his head, gasping to inhale. "Geez, fella, couldn't you've asked for the hotel's dough before you crushed my jewels?"

"Mind who you're calling fella, mister." Displaying her thick forearm, the husky attacker drew her shoulders back and sucked in her gut.

"Sorry," he said, noticing the woman's beige romper.

"I don't give a rank toot for your jewels or the hotel's dough."

"You after my wallet?"

"I'm not robbing you, stooge. Your consort, that runaway, is worth more than any cash you likely don't have."

"How you figure?"

"I don't. My boss in Birmingham does."

Cotton massaged the side of his head, kneading his fingertips deep into his temple, estimating how long Bobby Blount's private detective had been pursuing his habits and his haunts.

"I'm Mildred Ellis, but we won't fuss with handshakes," she said with a huff. "Where's the girl off to with the Irishman?"

"I have no idea."

"My purpose is to get that delinquent back to Scots Station."

"That's not as simple as it sounds."

"I watched you bribing that uppity spook. You a pimp or a peddler? That no-account Mick taking your steady sweetheart on a dinner date?"

"Why should I tell you?"

Ellis punched him in the forehead with an open palm fist. "That's why."

Cotton covered his face, allowing the pain to have its moment.

"And you can't afford a city cop to come peddling by, Captain Arnold."

"I haven't seen a warrant."

"I can you show you this," Ellis said, pointing her elbow at the bridge of Cotton's nose.

"I've seen that."

"Would five-hundred bucks set you square?"

"Five hundred for a tip?"

"Blooey on that, you earn it. You assist in her capture."

Ellis's sharp cheeks and blade-nose reminded Cotton of a sergeant he served and survived in France. The fifty he was carrying to pay Arch wouldn't corrupt her choices. "I need a drink for this one," Cotton said, motioning with his head towards his trunk. If Zach Hinton got Molly back to Perry County, she'd never know her God-given rights again, whether she ended up whoring at his lodge, working forced labor at the Wetumpka mill, or buried in the same burn pit as her daddy. He took a long, deep breath. "You wanna pop?"

"Don't touch the stuff, and you ain't either." Bouncing back on her heels, she removed a tiny pistol from her vest pocket. She aimed the semi-auto blowback gun at Cotton's face. "Where's the girl?"

Left on her own, Molly would be lost in Alabama or hooked up with Houlihan, until the Irish gambler tired of the burden. She and Cotton had been linked since he'd redeemed her family debt as a ransom dowry. If Lucius Arnold's archaic quotes from one of Shakespeare's peculiar Trojan War plays were valid, and honor was truly more precious than life, then busting into an opium den demanded virtue. His father believed that Luke dying in service was decent. Doing the same was his only paternal promise for redemption. It wouldn't hurt to have a spare gun to screw up Cotton's courage to the sticking place. "At the docks."

"Where?"

"*Shanghai Dragon.*"

"Some special sweetheart she is," Ellis said with the snort of a schoolyard bully.

"She and Monk are blowing down the road." The pain dogged Cotton's jaw. "Let me fetch my pistol. We can trek down there together."

"Nah, close by the train station, near the chinks' cathouse there's prime surveillance parking."

"You driving?"

"You are," Ellis waved her pistol in front of Cotton. "You and your roadster are coming to her rescue."

"I'd feel a heap better rushing an opium joint with my

Smith & Wesson in hand."

"We ain't rushing nothing. Who went into a place has gotta come out, in some form or fashion."

Rubbing the back of his neck, Cotton stepped towards the LaSalle's driver side, but then stopped. "Would you at least pay the reward money upfront?"

"Move it, wisenheimer," Ellis said, banging the side of Cotton's skull with another palm-fisted punch.

Chapter 40

The fragrant stream of a recorder flowed throughout the red flicker of the glass lamps. Between the gaps in the flute's lush notes, groans of pleasure flooded the couch. The pipe boy had prepared Molly a second bowl; each step and each instrument—the pellet, the needle, the flame, the bowl, and the long stem pipe—were vital to the ceremony. *Da yen* was all he'd said as she'd inhaled the perfumed smoke and exhaled a hazy cloud. The long, sweet groans grew louder. Lying on her side, facing a blue and white ceramic tea tray, she sensed the shrouded span of the entire room, like a sparrowhawk perched on a ceiling beam. Near the curtained entrance, a group of men reclined in a semi-circle fronting her padded couch. Tucked behind Molly, half-kneeling, Monk supported her raised top leg with his thigh and rubbed her thick mound of pubic hair, rocking his lower torso against hers. She released another guttural moan, emanating from deep in her abdomen. Reaching behind her, Molly stroked him, passing her fingers over the marble edge of his lower back. After the spidery pipe boy's second bowl, her panting carried her into a trance, the slender Irishman's warm breath swept down the nape of her neck. The droopy group of men flipping white tiles raised their heads like a six-headed snake when she howled again. She groped at Monk's buttocks. God had dumped her in this paradise. Another pair of hands greeted her. The Lord had given her men and granted her blessings. She was not lost. Molly latched onto the tender hands, dragging them to her breasts.

"The lotus flower want my sing-song girl?" an older Chinaman asked Houlihan.

Monk nodded. "And tell the kid to prepare another bowl, *yen chiang*," he replied, maintaining his thrusting rhythm. "Watch you aren't filling it with dross."

"It's all worth more than the price." The hunchback clapped his hands over his head, hollered a string of shrieking commands, and kicked at the dozing pipe boy.

The delicate girl slid over Monk. Her moon face covered with a glaze of waxen white powder. Fixing herself between Molly's parting legs, her almond eyes twitched with a fever.

Stretching the black tar, the boy's disciplined hands worked the needle over the flame.

The streaming trestle of ebony hair veiled the girl's moves, but Molly's lusty moans grew louder. Alma Mae never had the faith to believe. She always doubted the next sunrise, but her jubilee would last for years, a lifetime. Monk stood next to the couch, admiring her heaving breasts. Molly had snared him. All she had to do next was gut and skin him. The skinny Irishman had been in such a rush to get high and start sporting that he'd left his billfold sticking up out of his suit coat. When he passed out, she'd nab his dough.

The pipe boy pushed the small round ball into the bowl, stoking the gooey pellet over the lamp. "*Yen chiang*," he said, extending the smoking pipe to Houlihan.

In her vision, on the ride to the *Shanghai Dragon*, the woman's hair was the same lustrous black as the sing-song girl's. She'd intended to ask Monk if the pale woman with the dark braid was his wife, but she didn't want to spoil their illusion. He was delighting in his lopsided view of her swooning twist and folds, unaware of the price to be paid for the prize. Let her prey have his last glimpse of the will-o'-the wisp.

Monk puffed on the long-stemmed pipe and collapsed back onto to the couch.

The swaying boy offered the pipe to Molly, but the sing-song girl rose up, balancing on the side of the couch. "*Yen chiang*," she said, clutching his hand and steering the ivory mouthpiece towards her trembling lips.

The gnarled Chinaman unsheathed a walking stick from inside his loose trousers and smacked the tender girl's shoulders, knocking her to the floor. The pipe boy scurried to his pallet in the corner as the old man continued to beat the cowering girl. The cane rattled after each blow. From her crouched position, the girl lunged at her attacker. He backpedaled away, and her sudden thrust was halted. She crashed into a heap. Lifting up her leg, she clawed at the shackle around her ankle.

From the end of his bamboo walking stick, the old man produced a thin sword.

The recorder stopped.

The scowling hunchback placed the pointy tip of the long, foil blade against the flailing girl's upper neck until she was calm.

Propping herself up on the couch, Molly fought her murky high. She traced the rusty links of the girl's leg iron to a metal eye fastened to a floorboard.

"Don't worry, sweet treasure," the old man said to Molly.

The tainted cloud of opium smoke strangled her. The shrew at the rooming house had warned her, but like the gloomy pilgrims from the fog, she'd been trapped. Houlihan would pocket a bounty, and the hunchbacked bastard would chain her to the sing-song girl, sustaining her with meager tastes of opium. The vigor returned to her legs and coerced her off the padded couch.

"I'll cook you a special bowl." The old Chinaman sheathed his sword and pointed his walking stick at Molly.

Edging toward the entrance, Molly held up her palms.

The murmuring sing-song girl clung to the bottom of the

old Chinaman's pants. Cursing at the shivering slave, he quieted her with a sandal placed across her throat.

Molly reached for Houlihan's overstuffed wallet. The billfold trembled in her hand. The hunchback slapped her knuckles with his stick, and the sting made her drop the wallet. The old Chinaman whipped her across the back, two or three times, but with each blow, she advanced toward him. Seizing the bamboo cane, Molly swung at the old Chinaman but missed.

From the pocket of his long shirt, the hunchback produced a dragon-headed derringer.

As he fumbled with the pewter hammer, Molly bolted naked through the curtained opening. She scrambled down the stairs to the main deck. The orange lanterns guided her down the gangplank to the docks. Waves lapped at the steamer's bow. She considered jumping into the river for refuge. A caboose whistle let out a shrill wail, and she ran along the water's edge towards the depot. Not more than two-hundred yards away from the *Shanghai Dragon*, Molly grew winded. She bent over at an angle and swore aloud. Naked and alone on the wharf, she'd left her handbag onboard. Between gasp, she cussed louder and longer. She leaned against a wooden crate and sucked in more air.

"Don't move, Miss Lingo," a woman shouted, approaching from the depot and training a pistol on Molly. "I'm Agent Ellis from the Alabama Bureau of Investigation, and you're under arrest for the capital crimes of attempted murder, strong-arm robbery, and kidnapping."

"Kidnapping?" Cotton said, coming near with the woman. He walked past her, advancing closer to Molly.

"Captain Arnold, don't step any closer."

"She's bare-butt naked for Christ sakes."

"You gonna be a victim or a criminal?"

"Agent Ellis ain't a G-man, or any type of man." Cotton reached out to Molly with his suit coat.

"Stop what you're doing."

"She's been trailing us for a good while."

The agent's cropped hairdo and rumpled tan work suit seemed familiar to Molly.

"Earning that reward is your choice," Ellis said, aiming her pistol at Cotton.

"Just some oddball private detective hired by Hinton to ferry you back to Scots Station."

She'd seen at the train depot and the hotel lobby. She was the husky tipster who tried to warn her about the con artist while she was being used by a murderous son-of-a-bitch. That wasn't justice, God's or otherwise. The vengeance should be hers. The pain of retribution should be Hinton's.

"But she doesn't know what I retrieved from the LaSalle's front seat while she was napping." Cotton flung his coat at Ellis's gun.

The pistol cracked twice.

Yelping, Cotton grabbed his foot and hopped toward a stack of barrels.

Molly plunged her pilfered sword into Ellis's underarm.

The husky agent's eyes bulged out.

The blade bogged down in fat and bone.

Ellis dropped her pistol.

With an enraged howl, Molly clenched the handle tight and yanked the sword out. A red spurt covered them both.

Pressing her hand against her oozing armpit, Ellis rushed at Molly without care or caution and impaled herself on the blade.

Again and again, Molly rammed the thin blade through the lady agent's ribs, slaughtering a charging hog with a long caper knife. Each thrust stabbing through her breastplate, piercing her heart and lungs. Blood seeped through her work suit. Ellis slumped to the ground. Ignoring the blubbering rasps, Molly ransacked her pockets, uncovering a skimpy batch of dollar bills. She rolled the fallen woman into the water, and after watching the body float downstream, she tossed in the pistol and the crumpled bastard's walking stick. "Let's go," she said, covering herself with the suit coat.

Cotton draped his arm around her neck, and they hobbled off to the roadster.

Chapter 41

The window next to Cotton's head trembled. He'd noticed the loose pane when he'd walked through the apartment with the landlord, but for such a low weekly rate he couldn't gripe. Living in a shabby one bedroom flat on the Southside was a better deal than the digs across the river. At least there was only one set of stairs. The cracked and leaky windowpane jiggled faster, agitated to be stirred so long before sunrise; its mission was to bring in the light, not to keep out the late night din of railroad cars chugging towards the waiting mills. With a soft groan, Molly rolled over but stayed asleep. For the first week or two, she'd scrubbed floorboards and corners as clean as church marble while he promised her that Arch would come through soon. Cotton had driven to a Western Union towards Chicago and wired his poker money back to him a couple of weeks ago. His old army buddy had sent the dough back and then some, asking him to sit tight while he tracked down his steam shovel connections. A telegram would arrive any day now with instructions on where to go for the meeting, probably the Pfister hotel. The window's clatter grew louder. Cotton inhaled, his eyelids tightened anticipating the blast, but before he could exhale the bellow of the horn rattled the apartment. The slipshod Kraut landlord had to be skimming a couple of bucks off the rent. Flipping over to his side, Cotton allowed the train's hollow shouts to dull his foot's chatter. He had tripped the other afternoon on the uneven sidewalk in front of the dago row houses. The gabbing women hanging their husband's soggy long johns had snickered at his awkward fall, all but the one. Her breath reeked of red wine, but she'd allowed him into her front room to rest his feet and give his pitch, perhaps more charmed by his accent and his Gary Cooper style than concerned with her neighbor's opinions. Short and squat with curly black hair, she'd made the pretense of listening to his spiel on the benefits of owning McCorkle ceramic cookware, but they both knew she wasn't a buyer. He'd left the presentation off his call report, and started taking a different route to reach the VFW. Besides, he was earning more money plucking a few bucks off the aging warhorses down at the hall than he was peddling overpriced pots and pans to itchy housewives. They swapped stories about whores and wars from Manila to Havana while Cotton steadily clipped them for enough money not to make them sore. Selling door-to-door and gambling were more lucrative than a position at one of the specialty stores on the boulevard that Molly liked so much, stepping and fetching like some pencil-thin merchant at the five-and-dime. The passing night train's welter faded. A month or two from now, when they'd found proper accommodations, he and Molly would laugh about the time they lived in Bay View. Hopefully, the pane wouldn't crack and fall out before Arch's telegram arrived. The light rhythmic beat of the Westclox returned. Molly murmured, and he lassoed his hand around her hips, pulling her closer, trusting he could fall asleep before the rumbling thunder of the next locomotive.

Chapter 42

The first three or four times Molly had ventured to the park alone she'd gotten lost, but not on the way there. That was simple: left out the front door, cross over Euclid and Oklahoma avenues, daydream about arithmetic and Will Rogers, and then she was at the southeast entrance. The pavilion next to the lily pond, her favorite part of Humboldt Park, was on the opposite corner. After she smoked a few cigarettes on the bench, she'd head back to their apartment, but she'd wind up on Idaho St or Howell Avenue, and she'd meander home doubting every turn she made or didn't make. But now, after a month of daily trips to and fro, she only got lost if she wanted to be.

A crew of men milled around the wooden pavilion with clippers and rakes. City workers, but not colored like she'd expected, like Scots Station. Up North, white men did all the work, and if they had any Negroes here, they never appeared in Bay View. The grim pale Yankees would think Lizzy was a hoodoo woman, and Lord knows what they'd think of Sally's totems. One of the workers glanced over at Molly, and the rest of the group chuckled. It didn't matter what they said. She wouldn't have understood it if she'd heard it. A short trip to the pharmacy added new meaning to Pentecost's tongues like flames of a fire. She turned away from the crew's stares.

The mill's afternoon whistle sounded. It had taken a few days to learn the rhythm of the town, the flow of sounds. The city was never silent, but Molly welcomed the factory's steady toughness or the night train's offer of escape.

After the whistle blast trailed away, the crew collected their tools and marched off in a line as crooked as cows headed back to the barn for pails of bootleg Schlitz and sausage links that were for sale at the boxy public houses on the corner of every street in every neighborhood. It had taken them six or seven rambling days to snake their way to Milwaukee. She'd nursed Cotton's wounded foot, and he had held her through the retching, and the cramps, the twitchy sweats—nothing worse than bad stomach flu, the madam would've said. Once it passed, he'd taught her how to drive the roadster on a rutted road between two cornfields, and they began to make real time. She ground her cigarette out on the rough side of the concrete bench and slipped the butt back in the packet.

The pack of Marlboros was half-full, but she still kept the remainders. Saving tobacco allowed her to ignore the squinty-eyed leers of the landlord. He'd introduced himself as Mr. Schmidt, but Cotton called him Fritz. At the end of the week, Schmidt would knock on the door not long after Cotton left the apartment. He'd stick his beak-nose in the door and ask to see her husband, reminding her that Friday was payment day. She hadn't invited him in, yet, but she'd teased him with a flash of her garters, a loosening of her blue robe. She never knew when a two-bit handy or a sloppy suck would buy her a week's grace or a pack of smokes. The steel mill's whistle blew again, a short shrill for the start of the swing shift, and Molly rose from her seat. She wanted plenty of time to browse in the boulevard shops before she met Cotton at the diner. For the price of a dress in the boutique store window, she'd sport with the lecherous foreigner. The bright red chiffon gown would be worth enduring his sour cabbage stench, but she doubted Schmidt had a saw-buck to spare for a quick morning fuck.

At the northwest exit to the park, she spotted the cross on top of the gold dome and followed it towards Russell Avenue. Molly rounded the corner near the congested boulevard and the church. Cotton said Immaculate Conception was a Mick parish run by muddled Irish buggers, none of which meant a damn to her, but she couldn't make sense of why they were so dedicated to Jesus's mother. All Mary had done for certain was have a baby without being married, back in Scots Station that was no account for being named a saint. As Molly approached the cream-colored brick building, two women in black tunics and white caps came out the side door. Whenever she was with Cotton and saw the nuns, he'd make a crack about them needing a third, and tell a dirty joke about three nuns and a priest. The older one with gray wrinkling skin gave Molly a shy, porch cat smile and a tip of her crisp pointed cap, but the younger one with red blotches on her chin kept her rigid pout and stiff neck. Molly pulled down her soft cap and picked up her pace. Cotton had told her they were married to Jesus and could read your thoughts like scriptures. If they were that close to the Lord, then maybe they knew her floating nightmares of the beige coverall corpse bobbing up and down in the river, stuck under a log, churned up in a paddle wheel. She hadn't seen Rose since that night of impossible choices, each one more foolish and awful, as if Skillet or Alma Mae were guiding her mind in a game of mismatched dominoes. Molly didn't wear the rhinestone locket, hiding it the bottom of her shopping bag tucked in the back of the flat's cramped closet, but she could still sense her grandmother's shepherding spirit when the night train sped by and morphed her into powdery particles that disappeared with the racing draft.

Chapter 43

The Majestic Theatre was cheap, and it was dark. It didn't have downtown's refrigerated cooling system, and a few seat cushions were worn so wispy thin that the coils poked you in the butt, but when the house lights dimmed, and the music began, Cotton didn't care. Thoughts of scheming for money and Arch, or his father, his family in Georgia, faded as the flimsy canvas screen flickered with moving pictures. The newest films only played across the river, but the Majestic tickets were only a nickel, and Molly was a fan of anything starring Clara Bow. This evening she'd played a runaway actress torn between her love of the glamorous city life and the backwoods mountain man who'd protected her from discovery. Cotton never imagined himself as a dashing hillbilly, but in the darkness, Molly would grab his hand as the oily bad guy cornered whatever alluring young woman Bow was portraying this time. It wasn't *Macbeth*, but for a couple of hours nothing else existed; only make-believe was real. The pleasant spell of the darkness lingered as they strolled arm-in-arm, window shopping along the way to split a piece of day-old pie.

Continuing her recitation of the film, Molly stopped in front of the radio shop window, admiring the portable tabletop models. "I knew Clara didn't kill that man."

"I've got a chocolate pie feeling, or Boston cream if they have any left," Cotton said, peeking ahead to make sure the diner was still open.

"*Mantrap* was still a better picture, more believable."

"Apple pie would be OK, but not anything berry."

"Fritz plays his big old console radio all day while you're gone." A cardboard placard was propped up in front of the small cube-shaped RCA model offering easy financing and low monthly payments. "How's that work?" Molly asked. "That easy financing?"

"It's for suckers."

"Says who?"

"Says everybody that ain't a sucker."

Molly unlatched from the cradle of Cotton's arm. "I'd bear the cabbage for a proper listen to one of those music shows."

"And Fritzie's eyeballing?" Cotton asked before he thought.

"I've survived worse." Molly moved closer to the window. "Our plan doesn't exactly prescribe to starting easy payments for radios, or iceboxes." The Guinean bookie downstairs had just hauled in a dented icebox for his knocked-up wife. Since then, on most nights after the show, they'd stop at the appliance store. All the neighbors in their building knew them as Conrad and Margaret Luke. Cotton told new acquaintances to call them Connie and Maggie. Later, Cotton confided in Molly that Connie Luke had the same clipped alliteration and cachet as the famed baseball owner, Connie Mack. They were each accomplished at bloodying that bastard Ty Cobb.

"Starting 'em don't mean we got a finish 'em."

"Says who?"

"Says anybody that ain't a sucker." Leaning in, Molly pressed her forehead against the store window, a madly curious girl trying to pierce through the looking glass.

"That's a fine notion." Cotton stepped away from Molly and the frosty spring breeze biting his cheeks. The diner and the Majestic's marquee were the only lights shining on the avenue. If they didn't hurry, they'd be out of the pie, or he'd be stuck with boysenberry. But moving Molly along would be like Gary Cooper trying to coax a kiss from Clara Bow, everyone in the audience knew the racy starlet was going to reject the shy hero. It was in the script. "And it would make them easy."

"It'd all be easier when your beau does right," Molly said,

her words reflecting off the thick plate glass, transmitted like a news flash broadcast from the storefront window. "Either that or you peddle a few more pots and pans."

"My beau?"

"Or get better at poker."

"The diner closes any minute," Cotton pleaded, groping for his phantom pocket watch. He stuffed his hands in his overcoat.

"I ain't taking pie tonight."

"You know I hate rhubarb."

"I'm going home."

They each spun around, their bodies pivoting in unison, to watch the silhouette of a waitress—the hefty platinum blonde with too much rouge—dump a bucket of mop water, a wisp of steam rising from the curb. Cotton knew they weren't legally married, but it was simple to pretend—they were bound. "And I was gonna take you to Hollywood."

"Don't be too too loud coming into bed." With a clever grin, cheeky enough, Molly turned and walked away, pulling her velvet beret down over her ears.

Cotton whirled around, too, ignoring the twisting pain that spread from the ball of his foot to the back of his knee. He figured he could cajole blondie into an extra piece of the pie, or two, and that dates to the picture shows were a better cover than muddy straw and manure.

Chapter 44

On Saturday afternoon, returning to their walk-up, Molly chose the shortest route, hurrying past the barren sycamores lining Logan Avenue. The wind blew off the lake a few blocks away, and she cinched the belt on her polo coat, wishing she'd worn her cap. That morning, before he'd left for the VFW while Molly was still buried under the blanket, Cotton had patted her covered bottom and promised to bring her home a surprise. Climbing the drooping staircase to their one bedroom flat, Molly was pleased to have avoided their downstairs neighbors. Ada Marino was friendly, to the brink of meddlesome, and she was eight months pregnant, which didn't stop her and Enzo, her runty husband, from fighting or fucking most nights. She pushed the front door shut, and to block out the draft, she jammed a rolled-up bath towel, courtesy of the Brown Hotel, against the threshold. Cotton was in the kitchenette hunched over a wooden cabinet that sat on top of their table. He didn't look up from his tinkering. Skittering into their compact kitchen, she tossed her wool polo coat onto the living room sofa, whose boundaries encroached with their drop leaf kitchen table.

"Easy peasy, one, two, threesy, my fanny, lying-ass salesmen." Cotton turned the rectangular radio console around. "Cross your fingers."

"I'll cross everything." Molly sat down next to him and lit a cigarette. Cotton leaned over, and she tucked it between his lips. She lit another one for herself.

Cotton flipped on one of the many of switches on the front panel. "The tubes need warming up." He began fiddling with the knobs.

"Same here," she said with the suitable pinch of giddiness.

Once Cotton's foot had healed up enough, he'd been treating her to late night picture shows and a piece of pie at the diner on Kinnickinnic Avenue. Over a shared wedge of stale pie and burnt coffee, he'd alternate between vanishing to Havana and bragging about a promotion at work. Arch's steam shovel opportunity hadn't happened so far, but he'd landed a job selling showy pots and pans to the thick-browed foreigners in South Milwaukee and Bay View.

The radio began to whir to life. "Here we go—," he said. A soprano blared through the gritty crackle of the hissing radio.

Picking at a chip in the table, Molly listened to the nasally, high-pitched teenage girl croon about her Savior like she was pining for a sport with her sweetheart. She would have preferred one of the refrigerators they had on display at the appliance store next door to the radio shop. Cotton had argued they didn't need an icebox yet because it stayed chilly enough outside, which only reminded her that she shouldn't complain about the cheek-clenching cold that had her wearing overcoats in May and being unable to have a picnic in the park because it snowed in the springtime.

"Ada saw me carrying up the RCA." Cotton hooked his thumbs through his suspenders like a blue-ribbon winner. "She's bringing up Enzo and some stewed zucchini and greasy sausaes."

"Can you find less banjo and fiddle and more fun?" she asked, gouging her fingernail deeper into the flaw in the enamel table top. The only time she heard a long, drawn-out twang or smelled the salty aroma of frying gizzards was in the Negro neighborhoods around the meatpacking houses.

"NBC is broadcasting the Kentucky Derby from right there at Churchill Downs," he said like he'd given the RCA executives a golden ticket suggestion to sell more wireless units.

"Who's the favorite?" Confident Cotton had made a bet down at the VFW, Molly crushed her cigarette out in the ashtray. There was wagering and card playing at the lodge, but she didn't smell whorish perfume on his collars, and five or six nights of the week they let the Marinos know what genuine fucking sounded like.

"Whiskery, but I like Osmand."

"Funny name."

"She's better trained."

Molly spat out a fleck of tobacco. Cotton had dealt his pocket watch and the LaSalle, promising that once they were settled he'd make it right, and not in a cramped flat but in a real home. The Woolworth's shopping bag was packed for a fast retreat, no need fretting about it, but the city's never-ending modern consumption offered a tempting bargain. In Scots Station, you traded crops or livestock for dry goods. In Milwaukee, you bought what they manufactured, and they bought what you sold, all accomplished with a wink and a nod, like hustling a john up to the room, needing and wanting were treated identically. The madam would've prospered in a sprawling city like this, but not her folks. It would've consumed Skillet with opportunity. Alma Mae would've rooted out a way to survive like she'd done now, letting Stanley, with no one to read to him, sleep on the floor while she rutted with whoever demanded the least but paid the most. None of that accounted for much. They'd deserted her, or she them, and she'd keep swapping from one pocket to another until a day would come when she didn't feel like an orphan. A gust of raw wind rattled the front door, and the radio cut off.

"Goddamn contraption." With one hand on the table, Cotton lowered himself to the floor behind the radio, landing with a thump.

A chill nudged Molly's shoulders, and she wished her overcoat wasn't across the room.

"Until I fix this bastard radio, look what I found under your chair," Cotton said, holding up her necklace.

Molly grabbed the rhinestone locket away, believing its

appearance on the floor meant that Cotton had been in her bag, again. A sudden pulse of stress swelled in her gut, but a restful comfort overrode it, like the new peach blossoms outnumbering the boxwood bugs. Cotton prattled on about loose wires and lying salesmen, but to Molly he was talking somewhere else, babbling outside on the porch while another voice spoke to her inside her head, calming her in unspoken language. Slumping back in the wobbly kitchen chair, the same pleasant slackness of a dose loosened her arms, and she shifted into another place, a faraway field. Rose wasn't visible, but she was near, and Molly was tied to her as she'd always been, like the earth. They shared the kinship of seeds that sprouted from the same rich black soil. Together they grew, and they danced, spinning in a divine circle, their own pattern, forever.

Subscribe to Southern Fried Karma's YouTube channel, Fugitive Views, to see how Molly's orphan feelings determine her fate.

Afterword

About twenty-five years ago, my father gave us all a photograph of my grandfather as a barefoot knickered boy in Alabama. This late-19th Century reproduction served to crystallize the significance of Scots Station in our family lore. A lifetime of weddings, reunions, and funerals gave me sufficient knowledge of the land and the people, but for a better sense of the period I relied on *Cotton Tenants: Three Families* by James Agee and Walker Evans. My wife taught me a great deal about how psychic abilities are developed, plus I've had a few unexplainable experiences of my own. Sara Wiseman, author of *Divine Messaging for Beginners: How to Use Psychic Receiving to Guide Your Life*, gave me a clear explanation of one potential method to gain clairvoyance. To better dress Molly and other characters, I used an old Sears catalog and DK Smithsonian's *Fashion: The Definitive History of Costume and Style*. Shitty choices in college gave me an unseemly understanding of the effects of opioids, but I also used Jean Cocteau's *Opium: The Diary of his Cure*, David T. Courtwright's *Dark Paradise: A History of Opiate Addiction in America*, Thomas De Quincey's *Confessions of an English Opium-Eater and Other Writings*, and Peter Lee's *Opium Culture: The Art of the Chinese Tradition*.

Long hours peddling bulldozers blessed me to befriend a fine assortment of troubled gamblers and kindhearted rogues like Cornelius "Cotton" Arnold. Kenny Powell and Benji Deloach taught me several expensive lessons about poker, but I needed to round out Cotton's personal military history with Robert J. Laplander's *Finding the Lost Battalion: Beyond the Rumors, Myths and Legends of America's Famous WWI Epic*, Pete Cottrell's *The Anglo-Irish War: The Troubles of 1913–1922*, Thomas F. Madden's *Istanbul: City of Majesty at the Crossroads of the World*, and Lester D. Langley's *The Banana Wars: United States Intervention in the Caribbean, 1898-1934*. I enhanced my local knowledge of Ty Cobb with Charles Leerhsen's *Ty Cobb: A Terrible Beauty*. While attending the annual Pumper Show, I stayed at The Brown Hotel and discovered the historic district of downtown Louisville, and I augmented my experience with Gary Falk's *Louisville Remembered* and David Domine and Ronald Lew Harris's *Old Louisville*. Part of my knowledge about the Bay View area of Milwaukee comes from Ron Winkler's *Bay View*, but most of my understanding comes from riding late-night shotgun with Joseph Klugiewicz, a gentleman I'm proud to call a confidant and companion.

Acknowledgments

After thirty-plus trips around the sun together, I can't help but recognize the support of my lovely wife, Donna. She's not an editor, a proofreader, or a fiction fan, but her beautiful brown eyes and unwavering smile embody the love and devotion she's provided throughout this novel. My family has also been an essential element of this story. My children's encouragement, my parents' generous assistance, and my grandparents' grit have enabled me to create Molly Lingo and her world. I have also been fortunate to have the aid of my real estate investment team: Denny Carter, Alison McCondichie, Jesse Tanner, and Stephanie Tanner. They took care of business while I traveled away from the office or spent my mornings writing.

This is the first novel I've written outside the safety of my MFA pod, but it's not totally workshop-free. Two separate weeks at the Tinker Mountain Writers' workshop under the keen tutelage of Fred Leebron and Pinckney Benedict shaped this book in countless ways. Fred reads and writes prose like Bob Dylan strums his guitar, and Pinckney is the only person I'll allow to spit in my general direction to absorb his literary wisdom. I'm grateful to know each of you.

As all humble authors should do, I'd like to thank the Southern Fried Karma staff and their collective of editors and designers. April Ford, SFK Press Associate Publisher, has been especially supportive guiding Molly and me out into the real world, and Nicole Byrne and Emery Duffey have aided us in finding our audience. Cade Leebron and Eleanor Burden helped me put the final polish on the manuscripts, and Olivia Croom created an amazing cover.

Finally, I'd like to thank the Creator for bringing you and me together to share a story.

Photo credit: Davis McCondichie

About the Author

After 25 years peddling bulldozers around the globe, Steve McCondichie exited the corporate world to pursue his true purpose—telling thrilling tales about our meandering journeys through life. A rebel since kindergarten, Steve always gives the underdog antihero ample opportunities for redemption. A believer in the power of kinship, he enjoys examining how family shapes the individual and their choices. *The Parlor Girl's Guide* is his second novel. *Lying for a Living*, his debut novel, was published in 2017. A well-traveled native Southerner, he works as a real-estate novelist and lives in Newnan, Georgia and Amelia Island, Florida with his lovely wife, Donna, their four children, and five grandchildren.

Share Your Thoughts

Want to help make *The Parlor Girl's Guide* a bestselling novel? Consider leaving an honest review on Goodreads, your personal author website or blog, and anywhere else readers go for recommendations. It's our priority at SFK Press to publish books for readers to enjoy, and our authors appreciate and value your feedback.

Our Southern Fried Guarantee

If you wouldn't enthusiastically recommend one of our books with a 4- or 5-star rating to a friend, then the next story is on us. We believe that much in the stories we're telling. Simply email us at *pr@sfkmultimedia.com*.

Also by SFK Press:

Made in United States
Troutdale, OR
09/14/2023

12898896R00157